RULE OF THE GUN

On the run from the law, Vince M'Cloud and his gang decided to take over the sleepy little town of Arrow's Flight and use it as their hideout. After killing the sheriff, M'Cloud instituted a tyrannical reign of gun law, holding the town under siege. Anger simmered amongst the populace, and plans of revenge were afoot. But it was the appearance of the mysterious outlaw Abe Fletcher that really threatened to turn events around . . .

BRYAN SHAW

RULE OF THE GUN

Complete and Unabridged

LINFORD
Leicester

First published in Great Britain in 2000

Originally published in paperback as
Gun Toter From Kansas by Jed MacNab

First Linford Edition
published 2010

The moral right of the author has been asserted

British Library CIP Data

Shaw, Bryan, *1908 – 1960*.
 Rule of the gun.- -(Linford western library)
 1. Western stories.
 2. Large type books.
 I. Title II. Series III. MacNab, Jed,
 1908 – 1960. Gun toter from Texas.
 823.9'12–dc22

 ISBN 978–1–44480–093–7

Published by
F. A. Thorpe (Publishing)
Anstey, Leicestershire

Set by Words & Graphics Ltd.
Anstey, Leicestershire
Printed and bound in Great Britain by
T. J. International Ltd., Padstow, Cornwall

1

'I reckon this looks like what we want, fellers. Nice an' peaceful. Nothin' in it probably but a lot uv half-fried mugs who'll run like hell at the sight uv a brace of guns.'

Vince M'Cloud spat casually into the dust and then leaned on the saddlehorn to take a longer look at the town in the hollow below. He and his five companions were perched on a rimrock, looking down on a huddle of buildings and main street lying a few miles south of Cottonwood in Kansas.

The little town was too inconspicuous to be marked on any map; one of thousands of similar towns scattered about the Western plains. But it had one particular advantage for the men on the rimrock: it was only a matter of a mile or so from the main trail between Topeka and Dodge City. At regular intervals the stagecoach travelled that trail, and more often than not it carried gold ingots.

Vince M'Cloud, outlaw, killer, wanted in nearly every State, was looking for a quiet place to rendezvous — and this looked like *it*.

'Yeah, boss, yore probably right,' one of the men said after a while. 'Ain't likely anybody'll ever find us down there. Nice base fur operations against the stage-trail.'

'When we git down there yuh can leave the talking to me,' M'Cloud said. 'The folks'll do as we tell 'em, or else. None uv you mugs shoot unless yore told ter . . . Now let's go.'

He jabbed in his spurs and set his horse speeding down the slope in the evening sunlight. In a matter of perhaps seven minutes the main street of the town had been reached. The place was more or less deserted, except for a cowpuncher here and there lazing against the boardwalk rail. Nobody could have appeared less interested in strangers than these punchers. In fact, to Vince M'Cloud, the whole thing looked like a pushover.

He drew up his horse outside the Yellow Nugget saloon and dismounted swiftly. Then, with his men behind him, he marched between the batwings and came to a halt, surveying the scene.

At this early hour the Yellow Nugget had not gotten down to its usual run of business, but there were a few customers present at the tables — mostly cowpokes, half-breeds, and cattle dealers. In the distance, a redskin in check shirt and riding pants sat in inscrutable silence, smoking a clay pipe . . . As yet, the roulette and faro tables were deserted. In fact, it was the kind of setup which made Vince M'Cloud grin with satisfaction.

He jerked his head to his followers and strode to the bar.

'Whiskey,' he told the barkeep, and then summed up the few men who were gathered drinking. One of them, in tuxedo and white shirt front, a tall, blond man with an easy-going smile, had the stamp of saloon-owner about him. He came ambling forward, one hand on the crossovers he was wearing under his black jacket.

'Passing through, boys?' he asked genially.

'Mebbe.' M'Cloud eyed him. 'Depends on how much we like the district.'

'I'm Prentiss — owner of this place,' the blond man said, and held out his hand.

M'Cloud shook it perfunctorily, and then turned to his drink. It gave Prentiss the chance to weigh him up. M'Cloud was a massively-built man, over the six-foot line, with a ruggedly strong face. His complexion was a complete brick red from forehead to the roots of his hair. His eyes were blue, with much of the fierceness of a desperado. Once Vince M'Cloud had been an honest man, but women, drink, and a string of bad breaks had changed him into a wanderer — and a killer.

'Sheriff around this place any-wheres?' M'Cloud asked at length.

'Sure thing — right over there.' Prentiss nodded to a hatchet-faced man playing poker with a companion in a corner alcove. 'Why? Want him?'

'Not right now . . . ' M'Cloud summed things up. 'My name's M'Cloud,' he continued, watching Prentiss intently. 'I don't suppose yuh've heard of me?'

'Should I have done?'

This time M'Cloud did not say anything. He had satisfied himself that this town was so far off the map that his own depredations were not known. That made things a lot easier.

'Yeah,' he mused, after a while, 'I reckon I might stay around here fur awhile — What's the name of this place?'

'The town? Arrow's Flight. Usta be partly Aztec territory. Guess the only descendant of those days is over there.' Prentiss gave a grin and nodded to the immobile redskin smoking in his corner. 'That's Laughing Wind,' he explained. 'He's general man at the stores down the street. Harmless as a baby.'

'Pretty harmless-looking bunch altogether, if yuh ask me,' M'Cloud said, surveying — then his eyes rose suddenly as the batwings swung back and forth following the entry of a girl.

She was plainly not of the average run of Western females. She had a distinct air of refinement about her and neatly — even revealingly — dressed in close-fitting riding pants and a grey silk blouse. The orange kerchief set off her tumbled auburn hair to perfection. She was not exactly pretty, but she had a frank, open-air look about her.

'Swell-looker,' M'Cloud murmured, as his men stared with him. 'Now I *know* I'd like ter stick around. Who is she?'

'Chris Dawlish,' Prentiss answered. 'She and her pop run the Forked-J spread, 'bout a mile south of here. She don't usually come in here unless some important business comes up and she comes to collect her pop — Yeah, that's what she is doing,' he broke off.

M'Cloud stood watching. The girl

had stopped at the table where the sheriff was playing poker with his companion. Evidently the companion was the father, for he rose suddenly as she stooped over him, straightened his sombrero on his grey head, then, with a nod to the sheriff, followed the girl from the saloon. The sheriff sat back and lit a cheroot, looking absently across at M'Cloud. After a moment or two his gaze became more fixed and he seemed to be rooting in his memory for something. M'Cloud saw the look and turned away, preferring to watch the sheriff through the back-bar mirror reflection.

'I guess Arrow's Flight ain't a bad sorta place,' Prentiss said, reflecting. 'Bin here for ten years. Not a big town, as you can see — No more'n five hundred population, I'd say.'

M'Cloud glanced at his men significantly. Five hundred! Not much in that to cause worry, and most of them with their brains fried by sunlight.

'I'm footloose at the moment.'

M'Cloud said, his hand dropping casually to his right-hand gun. 'So it don't partic'larly matter where we an' my boys put up. All of us like wanderin' around and — Somethin' on yuh mind, feller?' he snapped suddenly, wheeling round from the sheriff's reflection and facing him.

'Yeah.' The sheriff latched his thumbs in his gunbelt, his eyes dropping momentarily to M'Cloud's levelled six. 'I guess I've bin tryin' to place you. Now I've done it. Yore Vince M'Cloud. There's reward-dodgers up and down the country, and in my office, with your map plain for anybody to see.'

Prentiss gave a start. 'You mean he's — '

'I mean he's a killer, a robber, and an outlaw. His last big trick was to hold up a stagecoach and get away with ten thousand dollars in cash. That was some time ago. Maybe the money's run out an' he's looking for more. How right am I, M'Cloud?'

M'Cloud met the cynical grey eyes

with a bleak stare.

'Dead on the nose, fella. What d'you aim to do about it? I guess yuh can't do much while I'm on the business end uv this rod uv mine.'

The sheriff hesitated, and gave a quick glance around him. The saloon was fairly full now, but that still did not help him much with the gun barrel projecting towards him relentlessly. So he went on talking, plainly not a man who was easily scared.

'I reckon it's my job as sheriff of this town t' run yuh in an' inform the authorities that I've got y' in jail. That bein' so — ' And suddenly the sheriff's hand flashed down to his gun.

Quick though he was on the draw, he was not quick enough. M'Cloud fired twice, his blue eyes glinting, then he stood watching as the sheriff dropped his gun and slowly keeled over to the sawdust. Astounded, Prentiss and saloon customers stared at M'Cloud. Such point-blank killing was a new one in the sleepy region of Arrow's Flight.

'I reckon this saves me a deal of trouble,' M'Cloud said at last, looking about him and still keeping his gun ready. 'You folks might as well know now as much as later that I aim to run this town in my own way. That's the one reason I came here. If any of you don't like it yuh know what yuh'll get.'

He nodded to his boys, every one of them with their guns ready.

'We're minus a sheriff,' M'Cloud went on, thinking. 'Just for appearances' sake I s'pose we oughta have one. I reckon Clint here'll make as good a sheriff as anybody.'

Clint Barcliff, standing next to M'Cloud, was a sharp-eyed, eagle-faced youngster with a sadistic grin. He gave M'Cloud a glance and nodded.

'OK with me, boss,' he assented readily.

'That's settled then. Somebody get the mayor,' M'Cloud ordered. 'Guess he might as well know how he stands, as well as swearin' in the new sheriff.'

'I'm the mayor,' Prentiss said, his

eyes still wondering. 'Seemed to the folks as bein' a good idea — me being the most important man in the town.'

'Y'mean yuh were,' M'Cloud corrected heavily. 'All right, swear in Barcliff here — an' hurry it up. Two of you mugs can be witnesses,' he added, to a couple of cowpokes at a nearby table.

Though the brief ceremony was an utter farce, and only performed at all so as to do lip-service to 'law and order', M'Cloud insisted on going through with it. When it was over and the star badge had been transferred from the corpse to Clint Barcliff's shirt, M'Cloud looked about him.

'I reckon a good lot of the folks in this town are gathered right here at the moment,' he said. 'That being so, yuh can take a message to those that ain't. From here on *I'm* running things, and I'll only stop being leader when somebody's quicker than I am on the draw. I'm an outlaw — an' know it. I'm also wanted for murder, so I don't care how many I wipe out, since I've only one life meself to lose. Got that, all uv you?'

There was silence, the men and women watching him fixedly.

'If any of yuh get the bright notion of ridin' outa town to inform the nearest authorities, my boys have orders ter kill. So don't try it . . . We're just one big, happy family in this place, and I'll only break it up if any uv you step outa line. Just go on with yuh business as usual and I'll not interfere. I'll live rent free in the best roomin' house in town — an' you, Prentiss, 'll see to it me an' my boys get all the liquor we need, on the house. What else I do is my business. All spying, talkin', and suspicious moves 'll have a bullet for an answer.'

Still nobody said anything. Most of the customers were, at the moment, too dazed to pass comment. M'Cloud gave a hard smile.

'Mugs, the lot uv yuh,' he decided. 'All right, boys, get this body outa here: it makes the place untidy. Bury it where nobody's likely t' find it. I don't want to have ter start explainin' about it if things ever get awkward.'

With that M'Cloud said no more. He finished his drink and then followed his men out of the saloon as they carried the dead sheriff in their midst. Whilst three of them used the cover of darkness to bury the body off-trail, some little way out of the town, M'Cloud went on a search for a rooming-house and finally settled on Ma Grimshaw's, across the road from the Yellow Nugget. Ma Grimshaw herself, big, homely, good-natured, was not at all happy at having six outlaws shoe-horned into her establishment — especially since they were not intending to pay — but there was just nothing she could do about it. Gun law had come to Arrow's Flight, and there didn't seem to be any way to defeat it at the moment.

To the folks who had normal business in the town, chiefly buying and selling of cattle and agricultural produce, the advent of M'Cloud as gun-dictator did not make much difference to them. He did not interfere with them. It was those who had to keep him and his boys in food and liquor who felt the sudden change in their fortunes.

But because he could shoot faster than anybody else, and also because he was utterly ruthless, M'Cloud succeeded in maintaining his position as boss, his boys loyal to him and watching every move the populace chose to make. Out-town trails were covered in case anybody got the idea of going for help. In a word, M'Cloud had the town in the hollow of his hand inside a week.

What he did with his time nobody seemed to know. In actual fact he was weighing up the district to decide the best point of vantage at which to hold up the next stage coach travelling from Topeka to Dodge City. When he had found it, and learned from various unsuspecting members of the Arrow's Flight community when the stage could be expected to pass a given point, he made his plans for action. The stage could be held up at Satan's Fork, a conveniently rocky intersection on the trail which afforded plenty of cover. But since the stage would not be due for another day yet there was time to spare — and M'Cloud rode out to the Forked-J. He had not forgotten Chris Dawlish, by any means.

The normal work of a ranch was going ahead when M'Cloud arrived in mid-morning. He had taken care to doll himself up more than usual, and he even looked passably handsome. Not that this fact impressed the dour foreman of the spread as he stood watching M'Cloud ride across the big yard.

'Howdy,' M'Cloud greeted him.

'You got your nerve,' the foreman said acidly. 'Get off this ranch before I have you thrown off. We've no time for killers around here.'

M'Cloud's expression changed. 'Plenty I could do to you, feller, for that — but I won't. I'm not here t' argue with a

hired worker. I wanta see Miss Dawlish.'

'She ain't in.'

M'Cloud glanced towards the ranch-
house. Just at that moment the girl
herself had come from the screen door.
She crossed the porch and descended
the steps to the yard. Then she came
forward, looking at the visitor curiously.

'Not in, huh?' M'Cloud gave a sour
look. 'Mebbe yuh'd better get yuh eyes
tested, brother.'

'I meant she's not in ter you!' The
foreman dropped his hand to his gun,
then hesitated as the girl spoke to him.

'You can fix up those cattle for
Murchinson, Larry,' she said. 'Dad says
it's all right — Good morning,' she
broke off, looking up at M'Cloud.
'Something I can do for you? I run this
ranch as much as my father does these
days.'

'This is M'Cloud, Miss Dawlish,'
Larry said, his jaws tight. 'The killer
who's taken over the town.'

'Any more of that, feller, and I'll let

yuh have it!' M'Cloud spat at him.

Chris Dawlish hesitated, then she motioned. 'Carry on, Larry. I'll attend to Mr M'Cloud — ' Then when Larry had reluctantly gone on his way she turned back to the outlaw. 'Well, what do you want here?' she demanded.

'You,' M'Cloud grinned.

The girl looked more puzzled than angry. She was better looking than M'Cloud had at first thought. Her eyes were violet blue, unusual with auburn hair, and she had an independence which appealed to him. Hard-to-get girls were his speciality.

'You want me?' Chris repeated coldly. 'Why?'

'Because I think you're the type that's needed to cheer up Arrow's Flight. I've taken the place over, in case yuh don't know.'

'I *do* know. I heard how you killed the sheriff and threatened all the townspeople. You're not welcome, M'Cloud, and you can get off this property before I turn the dogs on you.'

M'Cloud alighted from the saddle and eyed her. She returned his look, utterly uncompromising. He gave a glance over her slim but well-rounded figure and then grinned.

'Don't go gettin' high-an'-mighty ideas. Miss Dawlish, 'cos it ain't healthy to do that any more. You, an' your pop, an' lots uv other folks, have had things too easy fur too long. They want smartening up a bit, and I'm the man to do it — '

'By what right do you come shooting your way into a peaceful community and giving it orders?' Chris demanded angrily. 'How *dare* you, I say? Any more of this and I'll notify the authorities at Dodge City or Topeka and have you run in.'

'Won't do you any good. The trail's watched for anybody gettin' bright ideas like that. Anyways, you could have tried it before now if you'd had the nerve.'

'I'd no need to. So far you haven't interrupted things on this ranch. Now

18

you have it's a different matter.'

M'Cloud reached out suddenly and seized Chris's arm. She tried to drag away, but his grip was a powerful one.

'One thing yuh'd better realize, kid. You're as much under my authority as anybody livin' in the town itself — and if I haveta enforce that authority with a gun I will. I want yuh for only one reason — to be hostess at the Yellow Nugget.'

Chris stared in amazement. 'To be *what?*'

'You ain't deaf, kid. The one thing that Yellow Nugget lacks is a good-looking gal to make the customers welcome. Business would double if we could get that. I'm having Prentiss cut me in for a share of the profits in that joint, so naterally I want some kind uv attraction. And you're it.'

'Obviously you're crazy!' the girl said in contempt, yanking her arm free. 'I've this ranch to look after, along with my father. I never even go into the Nugget unless it's to find dad. What I said before, M'Cloud, still goes. Get away from here before I turn the dogs on you.'

She swung away angrily, but before she had covered a dozen yards M'Cloud's grim voice slowed her down.

'Which d'you want, Miss Dawlish? The job I've offered and your pa to go on living — or this ranch and his death?'

Puzzled, she swung back to him. 'What do you mean?'

'I mean that if yuh don't do as I say I'll make arrangements fur your pop to meet with an accident. And don't think I couldn't fix it, neither. I'm boss around this district, and when I give an order I get it obeyed, even if somebody gets hurt in the process.'

Chris hesitated for the briefest instant, then she turned on her heel and went back towards the ranch-house. M'Cloud called after her:

'I'll expect you to be at the Nugget at eight tonight, when I'll explain what I want. If you're not there yuh can expect plenty of trouble.'

He swung back to his horse, grim-faced, and rode out of the yard. Chris watched him go through the haze of the screen door, then she returned moodily into the ranch-house living-room. Her father looked up from the bureau by the window at which he was attending to business correspondence.

'Who was that?' he asked, puzzled. 'I didn't recognize him.'

'Vince M'Cloud,' Chris answered.

Her father looked at her for a moment, then he got to his feet angrily.

'What's that dad-blamed gunman doing on this spread?' he demanded. 'Where was Larry that he didn't clear him off?'

'I think he tried to, but I interrupted him . . . ' Chris thought for a moment, frowning. 'M'Cloud came here to make a demand of me, dad — the most preposterous I ever heard of.'

'What was it?'

Chris explained, and her father laughed incredulously.

'But the man must be loco!' he cried. 'What do you know about being hostess in a saloon? Anyways, you're not the type. It takes a hard-boiled gal to do that; one who isn't afraid of being pawed.'

'If I don't do it,' Chris said slowly, 'you are likely to meet with an accident, dad. M'Cloud warned me of that, and I'm quite sure he wasn't joking.'

'Bluff! You don't think I'm scared of that critter, do you?'

'I know you're not, but I do think it might be better if we both realized what sort of a man we're up against. M'Cloud's a killer, dad, and he stops at nothing. With his guns and those cut-throats he's got to help him he's made himself boss of Arrow's Flight and the surrounding territory. If his orders are not obeyed, he contrives accidents, shootings, and any kind of devilry he can think up. I've heard things from our neighbours scattered around. M'Cloud's been seeing them too, trying to cut in on their profits, and where they haven't been amenable there's been . . . an accident. Either we obey — or fight.'

'That's no longer in doubt,' Dawlish said. 'We fight.'

'With what?' The girl gave a sombre glance. 'The people of Arrow's Flight are just plain hicks with no idea whatever of how to handle gun law. You can't do it by yourself: and you can't get help either, because every trail out of the region is guarded. M'Cloud has everything sewn up in a neat little bag.'

Dawlish paced up and down for a moment or two and then clenched his fist.

'I thought once or twice about riding out to Topeka for help,' he said grimly, 'and this time I aim to do it. I'll get through. No owl-hooters of M'Cloud's can stop me. This guy's gotta be smashed before he gets too firm a hold.'

'No, dad, you mustn't do that.' Chris caught at his arm. 'It would be committing suicide. I think there's perhaps a better way.'

'What?'

'For me to take on this job he's offered — '

'What' You're crazy, girl!'

'No I'm not: hear me out. If I work beside him and give him the impression I like him he'll break down and tell me lots of things. The tougher they are the harder they fall. Sooner or later I might be able to find out the exact place where he has his men planted watching the out-town trails. Once I know that I can pass the information to you and you can go with the boys, locate the look-out concerned, and dispose of him. Then the way's wide open for you to go and get help. It's the only way to get results with things so covered with guns. We haven't even a telegraph we can safely use, remember — M'Cloud has it guarded. Only our own resources.'

'I don't like it,' Dawlish muttered. 'Sounds too much like walking into the lions' den.'

'It's the only way.' Chris had clearly made up her mind. 'I'll only be there in the evening, anyways, when there's no work to be done here. The sooner we realize that M'Cloud has a stranglehold on the community and set to work to beat him, the better. I'm prepared to use this job to advantage.'

'I still don't like it,' Dawlish said, 'but I reckon it is mebbe the only move we can make right now.'

2

So at eight o'clock that evening Chris arrived in the Yellow Nugget. It was fairly full of customers, fumed as usual in thick tobacco haze. She walked over to the bar where she could see M'Cloud and his boys were standing, not very far from the gloomy looking Prentiss.

'So yuh decided to be sensible, huh?' M'Cloud asked drily, as the girl came up, and his eyes dropped to the sequinned hem of an evening gown showing below her dust coat.

'Since it doesn't interfere with my ranch work in the day I thought I'd take a chance,' Chris replied shrugging. 'So I came over in the buckboard. What exactly do you want me to do?'

'Best thing you can do, Miss Dawlish, is leave while you're safe,' Prentiss advised, and M'Cloud gave him a sour look.

'Now, what kind uv talk is that?' he demanded. 'Yuh want this place t'prosper, don't yuh?'

'Not particularly. I get nothing much out of it with you and your owl-hooters cutting in on the takings.'

'Take no notice uv him,' M'Cloud advised, glancing at the girl. 'He ain't got no sense uv humour. As fur you, I'll show yuh where yuh can park yuhself. I had a dressin' room all fixed up for yuh. This way.'

Chris followed him through the saloon, glancing about her at the interested faces as she went. M'Cloud led the way along a back corridor and finally threw open the door of a rear room. It was fitted up with hanging wardrobe, a mirror with guarded oil lamps around it, and a few sticks of furniture.

'This oughta do yuh,' M'Cloud said, as the girl stepped in ahead of him. 'Let's see what sort uv a dress yo're wearin'. Bottom piece looks all right but I wanta see all uv it.'

Chris removed her dust coat and tossed it down. M'Cloud surveyed her bare shoulders and arms and the low cut front. He grinned in satisfaction.

'Good enough; 'bout time we had some glamour in the place. Doll yourself up a bit and then make yuhself nice to the customers. Yuh don't haveta drink — just as long as they do. Yuh'll be paid by the night. Five dollars flat and whatever yuh make on the side.'

'I don't need any on the side,' Chris answered coldly. 'I'm only doing this to protect my father, and for no other reason. The moment I find a way to get out of it I'll take it.'

'First find yuh way,' M'Cloud grinned. 'I'll see yuh when yuh ready.'

He went out and closed the door. Chris examined herself in the mirror and wished her dress had some means of concealing a small automatic. Since this could not be she finally finished her titivating and decided to take her chance . . .

And as she did so her father was also deciding to take a chance of a far more desperate kind. He was mounting his horse in the starlit yard, Larry standing beside him.

'No use, Larry,' Dawlish raid. 'This sorta thing can't go on. I'm having no daughter of mine makin' a play for a killer just to try and trap him. I'm going to get the authorities down here and take the risk of being seen doin' it. If I don't come back within six hours send out a search party — but not until. One rider might get by any look-out, but a party never would. If Chris gets too insistent on knowing where I've gone, tell her I'm over at Bob Tarrant's place. Not a word of the truth, mind, else she'll start riding after me.'

'I'll see to it, Mr Dawlish,' Larry promised. 'And good luck.'

Dawlish kicked in his spurs and the big sorrel bounded forward, passed through the yard gateway, and then struck the north-eastern trail for Topeka. He knew the risk he was running, but also knew that the hundred-mile journey was mainly across desert with very little chance for a look-out to hide. Had he decided to head for Dodge City there would have been passes to negotiate, where just about anything could happen.

So he rode hard under the bright stars, the cold night wind sweeping across his face, his eyes alert for the least sign of the unusual amidst the deserted wilderness. He had chosen the hour the mist had not yet evaporated from the ground. It hung in irregular bunches at intervals, usually condensed around tall tridents of saguaro cacti, or else it lay in carpets around the stately shafts of the yuccas. The Western night was as magical as always, with its tang of the desert and distant pasture-lands — but Dawlish had no time for beauty. He was thinking of Chris and her lone effort in a den of thieves to try and learn something which would establish law and order.

He was five miles out of Arrow's Flight and riding hard when he detected a break in the uniformity of grey white ahead. It appeared to be something dark — a mere speck at first, but it grew rapidly as he advanced towards it. He drew his gun in readiness, but there was no sound of a shot from ahead. The fact puzzled him, then as at last he came level with the dark object he saw it was an abandoned horse standing half asleep with no rider in sight.

Frowning, Dawlish drew to a halt, looking about him. At length he dropped from his saddle and went over to the horse, examining it for some kind of clue as to its owner's identity. He was intent on the job when a slight sound in the sand made him turn sharply — but not quickly enough. A gun barrel jabbed hard in his back.

'Keep yuh hands up, grandad,' a voice murmured — and Dawlish felt his guns taken from him.

'Turn around,' the gunman ordered, and Dawlish had to obey. He found himself looking at a shadowy figure in a black suit and sombrero.

'Not very smart, are yuh?' the gunhawk asked. 'I put me horse there as a decoy and then hid behind the dune yonder. An old trick, but a useful one. I guess there's nothin' more interestin' than a cayuse in the desert without a rider — Say, you're Dawlish,' the man broke off. 'I c'n just about recognize yuh features.'

Dawlish did not answer. He was intently watching his chance.

'The boss'll like to know about this,' the outlaw continued. 'I reckon he's makin' use uv yuh daughter, Dawlish, so it'll help a lot if yur outa the way. I reckon there's only one reason why yuh could be this far frum yuh home territory; yuh headin' fur Topeka. Right?'

For answer Dawlish dropped his hands suddenly and slammed out his right fist. He caught the gunman off guard for a split second and the blow crashed under his chin, sending him sprawling. Instantly Dawlish flung himself forward to seize hold of the gun which had dropped in the sand, but before he could complete his dive the gunman's boot came up with savage violence and cracked Dawlish under the jaw. He tottered, gasping with pain, then finished up on his back as a left hook sent him spinning off balance.

'Play games, huh?' the gunman demanded. ''Bout the wust thing yuh could try an' do, grandad. And I reckon yuh ain't goin' to git anywheres near Topeka, neither. I've got me orders to stop anybody who tries that. Yuh know the warning the boss gave: too bad yuh hadn't sense to heed it.'

Dawlish half rose, then he doubled up and crashed on his face as bullets tore into his breast. Another one imbedded in his skull. He became silent and the gunhawk looked about him upon the deserted wastes.

'Some mugs never learn,' he muttered, and putting his gun away, and Dawlish's two guns into his belt, he began digging a shallow grave. In fifteen minutes the only sign of where Dawlish had been was a disturbed area of sand rapidly becoming like the normal face of the desert as the night wind stirred the grains.

Satisfied with his handiwork the gunhawk took over Dawlish's horse beside his own and then settled down again amidst the blankets behind the sand dune. From here he could rest and listen. Any approaching rider would betray himself — as Dawlish had done even when miles away, the still air carrying the earthy thunder of hoof-beats for tremendous distances. But nobody else came riding, and the gunhawk muttered to himself as he thought of the night's vigil he had got to keep before being relieved by one of the boys at sun-up.

Meantime, Chris was at the end of her evening's work. She had spent most of her time talking to the customers and tempting them into buying all manner of expensive drinks — not because she had any interest in her task but because the better she was the more likely

M'Cloud would be to become amenable to her.

As the last of the customers began to drift away and she stood trying to stifle a yawn in the heavy atmosphere, M'Cloud came over to her.

'Just what I wanted, Chris,' he said, grinning. 'I reckon the liquor sales are up fifty per cent.'

Chris hesitated. Her natural inclination was to object to his free use of her Christian name, to make some kind of bitter retort; then she thought again. She had come here with the sole intention of worming into his good books, and the sooner she started the better.

'Just as long as you're satisfied, Mr M'Cloud,' she murmured.

For a moment he looked puzzled at the softness in her tone and the look in her violet eyes, then he put a powerful arm about her bare shoulders and hugged her. Chris hoped the involuntary shudder she gave did not register.

'Yore beginnin' t'get the idea, Chris,'

he continued. 'Just play along with me and things'll work out right — both fur you and yuh old man. I don't enjoy makin' people smart; it's just that I haveta protect meself. Here — take this fur tonight's work.'

He handed her ten dollars from the roll he had in his hand, and she looked surprised.

'You said five, Mr M'Cloud.'

'Call me Vince; it's easier. I'm payin' double for the risk yuh took. I like a gal who ain't afraid to take a chance. Later, mebbe, I'll ask yuh to take a different sort uv chance. But fur the moment it can wait.'

His arm dropped from about her shoulders and she stood thinking for a moment as she folded the money and tucked it in her dress.

'You know something, Vince,' she mused. 'I begin to think I may have been mistaken in you. You're not half so bad as I expected.'

He grinned. 'Wait till you know me even better, kid, then you'll really see how dead wrong yuh were . . . Anyways, that's all — for now. Go home if yuh wanter. I'd see yuh back only I want t'go through the takings with this guy Prentiss. He might try an' gyp me. See yuh tomorrow.'

With that M'Cloud turned away and Chris looked after him for a moment with a stony stare — then she went to her dressing room, put on her dustcoat, and in another few minutes was clambering to the driving seat of her buckboard. She was surprised upon her return to the ranch to find Larry, the foreman, still up and around, seated outside the door of the bunkhouse.

'What's the idea, Larry?' Chris asked in surprise, dropping to the ground as he came forward to unfasten the horses. 'Started working at night?'

'No, Miss Dawlish. I — er — ' Larry hesitated, then seemed to make up his mind. 'I'm waiting to see if your dad comes back.'

'*If* he comes back? What on earth do you mean? Where is he?'

37

'He went out to the Tarrant ranch to discuss business — but I'm leary. Y'know how things are around here these days with M'Cloud's boys on the rampage. I shan't have an easy moment 'til he gets back.'

Chris was silent for a while, her eyes fixed on the foreman in the light of the rising moon. There was something about his attitude, his tone, which was unconvincing. Suddenly she took hold of his arm.

'Larry, what's the truth?' she asked quietly. 'Dad hasn't gone to Tarrant's has he? He had no real reason that I know of: we haven't done any business with them for months . . . I want the truth, Larry, please.'

'Well, I — Honest, Miss Dawlish, your dad asked me not to say anything, so I — '

'I'll square that off with dad when I see him. Where is he? Gone for help?'

'Yeah. He said he couldn't stick the idea of you workin' fur a louse like M'Cloud just to try and learn something — so he set off fur Topeka about three hours ago. I'm to follow him if he doesn't come back in three hours more.'

'Why didn't you go with him? You and the boys?' Chris demanded angrily.

'We didn't dare. He said a party is seen quicker than a lone rider, and I guess that's true enough.'

Chris came to an immediate decision. 'Get your horse,' she ordered. 'We're taking the Topeka trail ourselves right now. The boys can stay in the bunkhouse in case of anything happening back here. Hurry it up — I'm going in to change. Saddle the pinto for me.'

She hurried into the ranch-house and was out again in ten minutes flat. Alarm had given her express speed. In riding kit, and well wrapped up against the cold of the night, she swung to the saddle of the pinto in the yard and led the way to the gates with Larry right behind her. Without exchanging words they hit the north-east trail and began riding hard . . . At first Chris found she had to fight intense sleepiness, but gradually the cold air revived her and she urged her horse onwards at the fastest speed it could make.

The miles flew by. Ahead, the view was clear, the mist having entirely vanished. Moonlight and stars had turned the desert into one sheet of grey yawning to the horizon, save where it was broken by outcroppings of cactus and mesa plants here and there. Then, far ahead, a black speck began to loom in view.

'What do you make that to be?' Chris asked quickly, straining her eyes in the uncertain light.

'Can't say rightly, Miss. Looks like a cayuse.'

'Yes — and it may be a trap,' Chris said. 'Don't go near it: work round to the back of it off-trail. This way.'

She swung her pinto's head and dashed the animal away from the recognized trail and into the loose sand. She kept in a generally north-east direction with Larry beside her, their horses' hoofs no longer echoing. Using the distant black speck as their focal point they began to make a wide circuit round it. It was not long before a second black speck became apparent, and not far away from it was a smaller object, clear against the light colour of the sand.

Chris wheeled her mount to a halt and turned quickly to Larry.

'Two horses and one man,' she said. 'No doubt of it any more. Obviously he's a look-out, but why there should be *two* horses I don't know. I certainly don't like it. I hope the second one isn't dad's.'

'Best go and see,' Larry suggested. 'We can work round on that jigger from the back. In any case we can't go much further in this direction; the sand's too thick.'

Chris nodded in the moonlight and they got on the move again. It was hard going for the horses as the sand became less firm. The only advantage was that they made no noise — but even so the crouching gunman became aware of both of them when they had come to within twenty yards of him. He jumped up instantly, clearly visible now.

Larry fired — and missed. A second afterwards a bullet whanged back at him and with a gasp of pain he toppled out of his saddle, clutching at his stomach. The thing happened so quickly Chris had hardly a moment to whip out her own gun before the look-out had her covered.

'Git down off'n that cayuse!' he ordered. 'An' keep yuh hands up!'

Chris slowly obeyed, dropping to the sand. She cast a glance down at the groaning Larry squirming nearby as he clutched his middle, then she found herself being disarmed.

'Very nice,' the gunhawk commented. 'Fust the old man and now his daughter — '

'What have you done to my father?' Chris burst out desperately.

'Done t'him? Shot him, uv course. Right now he's under th' sand an' that's where he'll stop. I reckon I can't shoot you down too because y'happen t'be the boss's partic'lar fancy. Wouldn't do me no good — '

Suddenly Chris lowered her hands and slammed out with her tight fist. Sheer fury and grief impelled her, and the gunhawk was taken completely by surprise. A fist blow from a slim girl was something he'd never expected. The fact that she was immune from a gun because of M'Cloud's orders gave her added courage. The blow she landed was not particularly powerful, but it did keel the gunman off his balance in the loose sand.

Chris followed up her advantage instantly. Flinging herself down on her face she grabbed the gunhawk's ankles and tugged violently, slamming him over on his back. He yelled with fury — and yelled even more as a handful of sand stung into his face, blinding his eyes and gagging his cries. That was all Chris needed. She ripped the gun from his hand and fired — not once, but until the chambers were empty. At every shot the gunhawk jolted and screamed, finishing up quivering, the life blasted out of him.

Chris remained where she was for a moment, trembling with fury and reaction, perspiration wet on her face. Never in her life before had she shot a man down so ruthlessly — but never before had she had such incentive. The thought of her father's murder had driven everything else out of her mind.

Presently, she slowly got to her feet again, leathered her gun, and took all the other firearms the gunhawk had possessed. Then she went over to where Larry was lying with anguish stamped on his face.

'I — I reckon that took care of him, Miss,' he panted, trying hard to grin in the moonlight. 'Best thing you can do is — is strike it out right now for Topeka. Don't bother over me. Nothing much y'can do.'

'Plenty I can do, Larry,' she replied, her voice taut. 'I've got to get you back home and to a doctor . . . You heard what that ape said about dad?'

'Yeah — Murdered him, I reckon.'

For a moment or two the girl was silent, looking about her, at the horses, the disturbed sand nearby which told its own story. Then she stopped and put her arm about Larry's shoulders.

'Hang on to me,' she instructed. 'I'll do my best to help you.'

Even so it took her a good five minutes to get the injured man on to his horse, and then it took him all his time to remain upright in the saddle. Finally she roped in her own horse, her father's, and the gunhawk's and fastened their bits on a single lariat. This done she swung to the saddle behind Larry and held him whilst she rode, trailing the other three animals to the rear.

She did not speak once, on the journey back to the ranch. Her mood was such that she could find no words. Only when the Forked-J had been gained did she break her silence, rousing the boys from the bunkhouse and giving one of them orders to fetch a doctor immediately from Arrow's Flight. Two other men she dispatched to the area where her father had met his death, with instructions to bring in his body in the buckboard, for decent burial. Another man she dispatched post-haste for Topeka with orders to bring help instantly to the gun ridden territory.

These details attended to she could do nothing but fret around the ranch-house for a while, doing what she could — with the help of the woman who did the cooking and general cleaning — to ease Larry's pain until the doctor arrived. Once this happened she had only time to think of her job as temporary nurse whilst the doctor removed the bullet. After that Larry was taken to one of the bedrooms.

'What chance has he, Doc?' Chris asked quietly, her face pale and strained in the oil light as the doctor packed up his bag.

'Every chance, Chrissie. He's tough,

and he'll pull through all right. What happened, anyways?'

'One of M'Cloud's gunhawks shot him down. In return I shot the gunhawk — not because of that, but because of dad. He's dead, Doc — murdered.'

'Your *father* is?' The doctor stared aghast.

'That's right.' There was a droop to Chris's mouth, but a hard glitter in her eyes. 'I don't think it was murder to kill the man who killed dad. Right now I've got one of the boys riding hell-for-leather for Topeka to get help. The trail's clear at the moment, so he can make it. This is only the beginning, Doc. If we don't smash M'Cloud now none of us will be able to say our souls are our own.'

'Guess you're right,' the medico mused. 'Anyways, don't you start taking any rash chances, Chrissie. I know I'm not your dad, but I do feel kinda responsible for you, seeing as I brought you into the world.'

Chris clenched her fists. 'There's only me left now, Doc, and I'm going to fight M'Cloud by myself if I have to — at least until help comes. If necessary I'll shoot him, too — tomorrow mebbe, or rather today, since it's long after midnight.'

'Watch yourself, Chrissie,' the doctor warned. 'You're up against a killer, and that's no job for a girl like you. Play up to him if you like, until man-sized help gets here, but don't start thinking about more killings. The mood you're in you might get trigger-happy before you know it.'

'I'm thinking of dad — and the vengeance I owe him.'

The doctor hesitated, searching Chris's weary, relentless features.

'Sleep on it youngster,' he murmured, patting her shoulder. 'You can assess things properly then. I'll be in tomorrow to take a look at Larry. Promise me you'll do nothing until then . . . *Promise* me!'

Chris hesitated, relaxing a little. 'All

right, doc, I promise. But that won't change my intentions, believe me.'

'Don't be too sure of that. Though you've had a mighty tough break I still think you've got sense enough not to make things too tough for yourself . . . '

On that, the doctor left the ranch-house. Chris saw him off and then returned indolently into the living room. She was just beginning to realize that she was nearly too deadened with grief and lack of sleep to stand up . . .

3

It was close on noon the following day before Chris awoke from a heavy sleep. She felt less keenly the savage anger of the night before, and as she dressed she realized that maybe the doc had been right. Until help came, the trapping of M'Cloud and the destruction of all he stood for demanded careful planning, not precipitate action. Yet how was she to play up to him and pretend ignorance of the fact that he had brought about the death of her father?

This was a problem which was still preoccupying her when the doc himself arrived, to pronounce after examination that Larry was slowly mending, though he would be out of the running for many weeks to come.

'What I can't understand,' Chris said, restlessly pacing the living room, 'is why there isn't some news from Sid — the man I sent to Topeka. He surely ought to have gotten back by now?'

In this she was right. Sid had had time enough, but there was a very good reason for there being no result. At the moment Chris was speaking, Sid was lying dead in the sand, not very far from the spot where the look-out had had his base. Around him, mounted, were M'Cloud himself and three other men, all his particular cohorts.

'Good work. Ace,' M'Cloud said presently. 'I guess yuh used yuh noodle fur once. Yuh heard shots, yuh say, frum your own lookout post, and rode over for a look-see?'

'That's right, boss,' Ace assented. 'It was moonlight, so I figgered I could risk it. I left my base on the other trail an' came to see what wus happenin'. I found Slick's dead body lyin' here, so I parked it on me horse and wus intendin' t'ride it inter town. On the way back I sees three guys. I follows 'em — safely. Two of 'em dug up old Dawlish, so I didn't interfere, but the other hit the Topeka trail. I caught him up and he said he wus goin' to Topeka fur help an' that I couldn't stop him. I changed his mind . . . After that, 'til daylight, I kept watch, but nothin' more happened. Then I rode inter town to let you know what had gone wrong. I daren't move frum watchin' both trails 'til I wus relieved by Shorty here.'

M'Cloud gave a slow nod.

'Frum the look of things,' he mused, 'the Dawlishes have bin makin' a mighty tough effort to git help — but we've crushed it good and hard. An' we'll go on crushin' it. Sure the gal will be put out, but her old man shouldn't go tryin' funny business. Anyways, I'll deal with her later. Right now, Ace, you an' me has gotta job t'do. The stage is due through in an hour on the Dodge City trail, and from what I can make out there's a ten thousand dollar gold consignment on it. We're goin' t'get it. Carry on here, Shorty, an' you, Lefty, go an' watch that other trail. C'mon, Ace, or we may be late.'

M'Cloud swung round his horse's head and began riding hard with Ace beside him. That Ace had been on guard all night, and was now roped in for a stage holdup, didn't make any difference to M'Cloud. He needed one reliable helper, and tired or otherwise, Ace was the only man. So they rode together along the sandy trails until finally they had reached the point already decided upon where an outcropping of rocks, first sign of the foothills of the distant mountain range, gave them cover from the sun-drenched trail up which the stage was shortly due to come.

'Mebbe thirty minutes yet,' M'Cloud said, with a knowledgeable glance towards the sun. 'Fur once we can relax. Grab some shut-eye if yuh wanter. I c'n keep watch.'

Ace nodded and settled with his back to the rock. For a while he dozed, so complete was his power of detachment; then he awakened again as M'Cloud gave him an unceremonious kick on the leg.

'Git yuhself masked,' he ordered. 'Here it comes.'

Ace pulled up his 'kerchief — as M'Cloud had already done — and then tugged down his hat brim. Taking his guns from their holsters, he stood waiting directly behind M'Cloud as the stage came into view, dust rising from its rattling wheels.

'OK,' M'Cloud said at length. 'This is where we move — c'mon.'

He hurried out of concealment and fired deliberately into the air over the heads of the stage driver and his ramrod. They made frantic grabs at their weapons, but another shot stayed them.

'Take it easy!' M'Cloud yelled. 'Stop the stage or the pair uv yuh'll be blasted down frum that seat.'

Grinding and shivering, the stage came to a halt, the horses snorting and the two men with their hands upraised.

'Just stay like that,' M'Cloud advised, then with a glance at Ace he added, 'Keep 'em covered. I'll do the rest.'

He hauled himself up on to the roof and quickly searched the luggage. There were a couple of travelling cases and that was all. M'Cloud's eyes slitted over his 'kerchief. He edged his way along the roof and looked down at the floor below the driving seat. Then he grinned to himself. A heavy metal box was by the feet of the ramrod, clearly marked — *Margerison's Bank, Topeka*.

M'Cloud dropped down to the ground again, seized the case's steel handgrip, and yanked it down into the dust. The ramrod and driver watched him, their eyes striving to pierce his disguise.

'Don't let 'em go yet,' M'Cloud ordered Ace. 'Make sure fust we've gotten the right stuff . . . If not we look further.'

He fired his gun twice at the lock of the case, blowing away part of the lid. With a wrench he dragged it up and revealed the gold ingots within. His guess had been right. The name and weight had been convincing enough in themselves.

'You'll sure get hell fur this,' the stage

driver shouted. 'Whoever y'are yuh'll be tracked down by the biggest posse yuh ever saw. I'm reportin' this when I get into Dodge City.'

'Sure do that,' M'Cloud said. 'Then start provin' who did it an' try an' find me!' He moved away from the case and looked within the stage itself. The only passengers were a couple of harmless women who obviously were not worth bothering about. He studied them for a moment as they withdrew sharply from the open window — then he fired his gun into the air.

'On your way, fellers,' he ordered. 'Pleasant trip.'

The men lowered their hands — the driver to the reins and the ramrod to the brake lever. They both knew better than to reach for weapons. M'Cloud stood watching the dust settle as the stage got on its way, then he returned to the box and contemplated it, his 'kerchief pulled back into place.

'Very nice,' Ace commented, coming over.

'Yeah. If my infurmation's right, there's ten thousand in gold here.'

'Good enough. Where do we put it?'

M'Cloud glanced up, his mouth hard. 'Whadda ya mean, where do *we* put it? This is *my* gravy, feller, an' I know how ter look after it.'

'Now wait a minnit, boss. I've taken as much risk as you in gettin' this stuff an' I want a — '

'Shut up! Yuh'll get a cut, don't you fret, but not right now. We need more'n this before we start movin'. Gotta let the heat die down fust. 'Sides, there'll be more gold sent this way afore we're through. When I'm good an' ready I'll split the total between us. Until then I'm hiding it.'

'Where?' Ace's face was suspicious.

'That's my business. Yuh can scram back to town. I'll foller later.'

Ace hesitated, his hand dropping to his gun, then as he saw the look on M'Cloud's face he thought better of his intentions. He knew only too well that M'Cloud could outshoot him any time he chose. The risk wasn't worth it. But he *could* watch from a distance where M'Cloud finally hid the gold —

'And don't foller me,' M'Cloud added. 'I'm up ter all the tricks yuh can pull, Ace. If I see any signs of yuh around when I've found the spot fur this gold I'll shoot yuh down.'

'OK, so you don't trust me,' Ace growled, turning back to his horse.

'You an' a rattler,' M'Cloud told him, and after that he stood watching as Ace began to ride away, and he kept on watching him until at last the distances and the desert had swallowed him up. Thereupon M'Cloud buried the case right at the spot where he stood, knowing he was safe from being overlooked at this particular moment. He marked a rock so as he would know the exact spot again; then returning to his horse he too began the ride back to town, grinning to himself at the thought of being ten thousand better off. And nobody could ever catch up and ask awkward questions: that was the nicest part of all.

That the stage coach had been held up and cleaned of its gold consignment was not generally known to the sleepy, gun-bullied denizens of Arrow's Flight until that same evening, and then it was Clint Barcliff, the sheriff and M'Cloud's right hand man in the town, who made the fact known. In fact, he had no alternative, for the news had come over the telegraph from Dodge City, and as well as it being a message intended for the Sheriff of Arrow's Flight, it was also news for the people to hear. The man in the general store post-office who handled the telegraph, was not particularly quiet about interesting information when he got it.

'Who did the robbery we don't know,' Clint said, addressing the not inconsiderable gathering in the saloon. 'I've bin told t'keep my eye open fur two outlaws — one a hefty guy, and the other smaller. Nothin' t'identify 'em by. They was wearin' 'kerchiefs over their faces. T'my mind it's a waste uv time thinkin' about it — but that's the tip off. If any uv yuh hear anythin' interestin' just come along to my office.'

He turned back to the bar and gave a sly glance at M'Cloud. M'Cloud grinned.

'Nicely put, youngster,' he murmured. 'I reckon the Dodge City authorities don't know yuh've replaced the former sheriff. I s'pose they'd drop dead if they knew yuh was cahoots with the very guys who'd pulled that robbery . . .'

'An' hidden the proceeds in a secret cache some place,' Ace remarked, putting down his empty brandy glass.

'Keep yuh lip buttoned, you,' M'Cloud spat. 'One word outa line an' not only me, but you as well'll be in plenty uv trouble. Stop beefin': yuh'll get yah cut in due time.'

'We all will,' Clint Barcliff said, still smiling. 'I don't s'pose yuh'd try gyppin' us, boss, would yuh?'

M'Cloud gave him a quick, hard

glance — then he looked up sharply as through the batwings came Chris Dawlish. She was dressed in sombre black riding clothes, the only relief being a check mackinaw as protection from the night cold.

'Here comes trouble uv a different sort,' Clint commented. 'I'll gamble that dame's plenty sore at the murder uv her pop.'

Catching sight of M'Cloud at the bar, Chris walked across to him. Her face was very pale, violet eyes expressionless. When she reached M'Cloud she paused before him, studying him.

'Howdy. Chris,' M'Cloud said, grinning. 'Here fur the usual night's work?'

'Pretty obvious I'm not, isn't it?' Her voice stung with venom. 'I've no evening dress on, and I'm only staying long enough to tell everybody what I think about you.'

'Yeah?' M'Cloud measured her, an eyebrow raised.

'Last night,' she continued deliberately, 'one of your men shot down my father — murdered him. He was buried this morning in the chapel church yard. Most of the people know by now that he was murdered, but not all of them know who by. I'm telling them — right now.'

Chris looked tearfully at the assembly around her. Some of them looked at M'Cloud, others at their beer glasses.

'In return I shot the man who killed my father,' Chris continued. 'That's justice! An' I — '

'I'm mighty sorry fur what's happened, Chris — mighty sorry,' M'Cloud interrupted, and he managed to look genuinely contrite. 'Naterally, you did right in shootin' the critter who committed murder — but I reckon yuh pa should have remembered that I gave warning of what would happen if anybody tried t'leave town. My man was only following out orders. He was a no-good, anyway, so if yuh killed him I can't see it matters.'

'Clever, aren't you?' Chris asked bitterly. 'Trying to swing things round so you look like the big-hearted boss! A gun in one hand and tears in your eyes. I've only one answer for the thing you did, M'Cloud, and it's this — '

Her hand flashed up suddenly from the pocket of her riding skirt and a gun glinted. Instantly M'Cloud threw his brandy straight into her face. She gasped, blinded by the spirit, and Clint snatched the gun from her hand. Several of the men rose up from their tables as though to help her, but Clint kept on holding the gun, turning it on them.

'Better not,' he advised.

Chris wiped her smarting eyes and blinked furiously. The next thing she knew was that M'Cloud's arm was about her shoulders.

'I reckon yuh wouldn't be nateral if yuh didn't feel sore at yuh father's death,' he said, 'but honest, Chris, didn't have anythin' t'do with it. I gave yuh my word nothin' would happen to yuh dad if you worked for me — and nothin' did, fur as I was concerned. Yuh dad took too big a risk. Don't go spoilin' things, Chris. Last night, yuh said that mebbe yuh had me figgered wrong. I'm hopin' yuh still feeling that way. An' I'm sorry 'bout throwin' the brandy in yuh face. Had to protect myself, I reckon.'

For a moment or two Chris did not answer. So far everything was working out as she had planned it. She still had it in mind to play alongside M'Cloud until by accident or design she had something on him which could nail him for good — but for her to have walked in the saloon all smiles and shown no regrets at the death of her father would have been too obviously unconvincing. As things stood now she had deliberately blown her top: now she could swing round without it exciting M'Cloud's suspicions.

'I — I suppose it wasn't really *your* fault,' she said slowly.

''Course it wasn't. I gave warnin' and if it ain't heeded I can't help it, no matter who it is ... Have a drink,

Chris, then mebbe yuh'll feel better.'

'Well . . . just this once.' She dabbed at her still watering eyes and stood thinking as M'Cloud handed her a brandy. Clint Barcliff stood watching her in dour suspicion. Ace, on the other side of M'Cloud, was frozen faced, the memory of hidden gold still chasing through his killer's brain.

'Better?' M'Cloud asked at length, grinning, and Chris nodded.

'I — I guess so.'

'Then how's about doing yub job as usual? Or is it too much to ask after buryin' yuh old man?'

'Nothing I can do can bring him back,' Chris sighed. 'That wouldn't make any difference — but I'm not dressed for it.'

'Don't matter fur this once. Just leave off the mackinaw and th' rest uv yuh's fine.'

Chris thought about it for a moment, then she seemed to make up her mind. With a nod she turned away and headed in the direction of her dressing room.

'Simple,' M'Cloud murmured, pouring himself another drink. 'I reckon I can handle wimmin as easily as horses — an' give me that hardware, yuh lug,' he added, snatching the gun from Clint.

Clint shrugged and rubbed his chin thoughtfully, then Ace made a comment.

'Yuh a sucker, boss,' he said drily. 'That dame's takin' yuh for a ride and yuh don't know it. I can tell by th' look in her eye. Before yore finished yuh'll — '

Ace got no further. M'Cloud's fist suddenly crashed straight into his face and knocked him sprawling in the sawdust. He hit the back of his head on the brass cuspidor and winced.

'Next time yuh start tellin' me how ter handle me affairs, think again,' M'Cloud snapped. 'Yuh gettin' too big fur your boots, Ace.'

'Yeah?' Ace rubbed his throbbing jaw and then began to slowly scramble to his feet. As he did so he turned away from M'Cloud and yanked out his gun.

Swinging round abruptly, he fired — but the bullet was a fraction out of line. It struck the whiskey bottle at M'Cloud's elbow and splintered it to fragments, drenching M'Cloud's sleeve in spirit. He had his own gun out instantly.

'All right, fire!' Ace invited venomously. 'What th' heck do I care? Yuh'll only gyp the lot uv us afore yore through — includin' the gold yuh stole from that coach today.'

'You dirty liar!' M'Cloud grated at him. 'Keep yuh trap shut, Ace, before I let yuh have it.'

'Buryin' it all fur yuhself!' Ace yelled. 'That's what yuh doing! So's yuh can walk out when yuh feel like — '

'Why, you — '

The hamimer on M'Cloud's gun drew back, and simultaneously a shot exploded from somewhere in the middle of the saloon. The bullet blasted the gun clean out of M'Cloud's hand without hurting him, and then splintered the back bar mirror into fragments.

For an instant there was a dead silence. M'Cloud turned slowly, in utter wonder, astounded to find his hand in one piece.

His gaze rested finally on a lean-faced youngish man seated at a centre table, a glass of rye on one side of him and a .38 in the other. He had its barrel resting on the edge of the table and apparently had fired from that position — which said plenty for his marksmanship.

He grinned a little and put his gun away. Then he stood up. He was perhaps a little short of six feet and thick in the shoulders. He slouched more than walked as he came over to the bar. He had the burned-in-brown skin of an outdoor man, and his dusty check shirt and pants stamped him as just another saddletramp.

'Bit quick on the draw, M'Cloud, ain't you?' he asked drily, his thumbs now latched in the belts of his crossovers.

M'Cloud swallowed hard, then glared. 'What the hell d'you think yuh doin', bustin' in on my affairs? An' how d'yuh know my name?'

'Advertised plenty, ain't it, up and down — with your mug to match. I couldn't forget that face any place.'

Clint gave a dry grin and then let it fade as M'Cloud looked at him. Ace struggled to his feet and dusted the sawdust from his clothes. He picked up his gun and leathered it.

'Thanks, feller, anyway,' he said briefly. 'I guess yuh saved me from being plugged.'

'Honour among thieves mebbe,' the newcomer reflected. 'I can only think you're a bit impulsive, M'Cloud. Doesn't do if yuh want t'keep your men.'

'This guy talked too loud,' M'Cloud snapped.

'Sure — sure, we heard him. All about you robbin' the stage coach and hiding the gold . . . '

The newcomer broke off as Chris suddenly came up in the rear, her auburn hair freshly brushed, the mackinaw removed to reveal her black silk blouse.

'Vince, is this true about the stage?'

she demanded. '*Did* you rob it?'

'No,' M'Cloud growled. 'Ace is talkin' outa turn.'

'Like hell I am,' Ace snapped. 'He held up the coach, along with me, and then buried the gold some place where only he can find it. I think it's a double cross!'

With that he turned away, not caring to risk further trouble. The girl looked after him, then back to M'Cloud.

'Nothing yuh can do about it, Chris,' he said. 'Ferget it. Only bank gold, anyways, and who cares about a bank?'

Chris looked at him for a moment, her expression hard to understand. Then she looked at the newcomer. He had hard grey eyes and a thin-lipped mouth. The way he looked at her made her feel about four feet tall.

'Name's Fletcher,' he said brusquely. 'Abe Fletcher. I'm just passin' through from Oklahoma way . . . I like your looks, kid. What's the name?'

'None of your business,' M'Cloud told him. 'Get on with your job, Chris.'

She gave Fletcher a studied look of her violet eyes and received his insolent stare in return; then she turned away and set about her self-imposed task of being a hostess. She hoped it would not dawn on M'Cloud that he no longer had any hold on her. His former threat that her father would suffer it she did not do as he asked no longer held good. Apparently, though, he had come to the conclusion that she was working for him because, deep down, she liked him. The more he believed that the sooner she might find out something. In fact she had a lever now — That gold. If she could find where it was hidden, and then get some of the saloon customers to declare what Ace had said in their bearing . . .

'Yeah, nice girl,' Abe Fletcher said, and went back to his table for the glass of rye. Returning, he put it on the bar counter and contemplated it.

'I ain't so sure I like your attitude, fella,' M'Cloud told him. 'No room around here for guys who express themselves too freely. I'm the only boss, and Arrow's Flight knows it.'

'Arrow's Flight being this dump, I suppose? Not much t'be boss of — not a man of your talents.'

'Don't take much talent to knock sense inter a lot of mugs like this,' M'Cloud growled. 'And suppose yuh tell me more about yuhself. Yuh passin' through, y'say? I can't allow that.'

'No?' The cold grey eyes were questioning. 'Nobody tells me what to do, M'Cloud.'

'This time *I'm* telling yuh — and yuh'll listen. It's queer yuh even got in the town without bein' blasted. I've men watching the trails for incoming and outgoing folk. I don't allow anything 'cos of possible law officers.'

'I wondered what that critter wanted when he held me up on the trail in from Oklahoma,' Fletcher mused. 'I put a slug through his left eye an' it didn't improve him. One of your boys, was he?'

M'Cloud stared as Fletcher finished his rye and ordered another.

'Yuh — yuh *killed* him, y'mean?'

'Sure. I don't like being intercepted.'

In the background, unnoticed, Chris had worked her way round to be within earshot, at the same time handing a nice line in smiles to a customer. She still had a riddle to solve for herself: why no help had ever come from Topeka in response to the man she had sent. She had gathered by now that he had been spotted somehow and wiped out, but she would have liked proof. She did not get it. Instead she heard other things — and they seemed to confirm her opinion of the ice-eyed Abe Fletcher.

'If I chose t'leave this district, M'Cloud, I'd do it,' he said. 'No owl-hooter with a six-gun would stop me because I'd get him first . . . Only mebbe I don't *want* to move on. I like the set-up yuh've got here. Nice and peaceful. Plenty of mugs to do the work an' none of them with the damned guts to stand up fur themselves.'

'Yuh'll make it easier if yuh don't move on,' M'Cloud responded. 'But in any case yuh not *going* to. Yuh might try and bring the law from Topeka or Dodge.'

'Who? Me?' Fletcher grinned cynically. 'I can see myself doin' that. I'm wanted as much as you are, M'Cloud. An' if you doubt it, take a look at this . . .'

From his hip pocket Fletcher pulled out a creased and folded reward-dodger. He spread it on the bar counter and M'Cloud looked at it in surprise. It depicted Abe Fletcher plainly enough, six-guns in his hands, and underneath was the wording:

$5,000 REWARD!
WANTED FOR MURDER!

Abe Fletcher, better known as the
'Oklahoma Kid'.
Aged about 28, 5 ft. 10 ins.,
grey eyes, black hair. Any information
to
Brant Mulligan.
Sheriff — Indian Gap,
Oklahoma.

'Me!' Fletcher said proudly, grinning. 'Yore not in this stage coach and killing business by yourself, M'Cloud. I ripped this off a trail board as I rode in from Oklahoma. I guess I made that State too hot for me.'

'Which means a law officer may come here lookin' fur yuh,' M'Cloud snapped. 'And that endangers me! Yuh've not bin very smart, Fletcher!'

'No? Smart as you have, I guess. Anybody know *you're* here? Course they don't. Nobody knows I'm here either — which is why I say it's a good place to stop for a while. You and me might make a good team.'

'Doin' what?'

'Runnin' things.' Abe Fletcher put the reward-dodger back in his pocket and his grey eyes strayed to Chris's back as she sat at the nearby table, absorbing everything. 'And sharin' things,' Fletcher added.

'I don't share nothin' with nobody,' M'Cloud said.

'Mebbe you'll have to. Can't pick an'

choose. I can help in lots of ways. In my time I've had a bit of education: it's useful sometimes. You're just a roughneck.'

'Why, you dad-blamed — '

'Save it,' Fletcher suggested, his right hand gun leaping into his fingers. 'We can either be nice or nasty about this. It's up to you.'

M'Cloud studied him for a moment, then he jerked his head.

'Better come to my office, Fletcher. We can talk a bit more peacefully there.'

'Suits me.' Fletcher re-leathered his gun and then his eyes strayed to Chris. Instead of following M'Cloud he moved to her and caught at her arm. She turned a startled face towards him. 'What I said about you, kid, still goes,' he said. 'I like your looks — and everythin' else.'

Chris tightened her lips as his insolent grey eyes went down her figure to her feet. She just could not help bringing up her hand and slapping him hard across the face. He took it without flinching.

'Even better when you're burned up,' he commented. 'Puts some colour in your cheeks. They can do with it.'

M'Cloud came over, his eyes menacing.

'Lay off her, Fletcher. She ain't your property. I'm responsible fur her safety.'

Fletcher shrugged. 'OK. But I still like the look of her . . . '

He turned away, and as he went the flat of his hand struck across Chris's shapely rear as she leaned over the table to resume conversation with the customer. She straightened up, crimsoning, but by this time Fletcher bad ambled away with M'Cloud. He followed him into the office and M'Cloud closed the door.

'We'll get two things straight fust,' M'Cloud said, sitting down at the desk and motioning Fletcher to do likewise. 'I'm the boss in this region, and Chris Dawlish is my especial girlfriend. Never forget those two things an' we'll get along OK.'

Fletcher did not commit himself one way or the other: he just gazed stonily.

'I s'pose yuh want to team up with me?' M'Cloud asked.

'Why not? I know too much about you t'do anything else. And you know too much about me. We're in each other's hands, M'Cloud. Either we split on each other, or we work together. I reckon that answers your question.'

'All right then — but yuh'll take orders an' obey them. Savvy?'

'As long as you're the boss, sure,' Fletcher agreed, somewhat ambiguously.

'Since I came here I've added a lot of boys to my side,' M'Cloud continued. 'I can trust most uv 'em, chiefly because they know what they'll get if they don't obey orders . . . Y'know about the stage hold-up so there's no point in hiding it. I did the job, with Ace, an' I aim t'do plenty more. I can do with a guy like you to help. Quick on the draw an' not easily scared.'

'When's the next?' Fletcher asked briefly.

'Day after tomorrer. I figgered we

might attack from a different point an' get the advantage uv surprise. Near as I can figger it over the telegraph there's a five thousand gold consignment being sent. Only half as much as last time but worth having.'

'I keep thinking of what Ace said,' Fletcher mused. 'About you hiding the gold for yourself. How true is that?'

'I've *got* to have a secret cache!' M'Cloud gave a glare. 'If any of the mugs workin' fur me got their mitts on all that gold there'd be blue murder! I'm keepin' everythin' hidden 'til I decide the heat's off an' we can check out. Then I'll divide the total.'

'Just as long as you do,' Fletcher said. 'Otherwise I might get into the same mood as Ace ... OK, so we rob the stage day after tomorrow. I'm with you. Meantime I want the same rights as the rest of your boys. Free lodging and drink. That's the understood thing, isn't it?'

'Yuh'll get it. Yuh'll doss at Ma Grimshaw's over the way. Tell her I sent yuh; that'll be enough.'

Fletcher nodded and remained seated, thinking.

'What happened to the guy you bumped off?' M'Cloud asked. 'The one guarding the Oklahoma trail, I mean.'

'I buried him deep.'

'OK. I'll send another man out there pronto.' M'Cloud got to his feet. 'Guess that's all, Fletcher. Yuh'll be around town or in Ma Grimshaw's if I want yuh.'

Fletcher nodded and without saying anything further he ambled out of the office and back into the saloon. He went straight over to where Chris was seated at a table, this time working on another customer. She glanced up sharply as she realized Fletcher was studying her.

'Do you *have* to keep following me around?' she asked bitterly. 'Leave me alone!'

'Where do you hang, out?' Fletcher asked. 'I reckon we oughta get better acquainted.'

'Yeah?' M'Cloud asked, coming up in the background. 'Are yuh fergettin' so soon what I told yuh, Fletcher?'

'No harm in talkin' to the gal,' Fletcher retorted. 'She's about the only decent looking one in this whole female community. You shouldn't keep a good thing to yourself, M'Cloud.'

He did not press his question, however. Returning to the bar he ordered a whiskey and as he drank it he murmured an enquiry.

'Where does the dame come from, Baldy?'

The barkeep glanced at Chris. 'Her? From the Forked-J, 'bout one mile or so south of here.'

'Thanks.' Fletcher raised his eyes casually to the bar mirror, then his gaze became fixed and his lips hard. Abruptly he spun round, both guns in his hands, and fired relentlessly towards the batwings.

The sudden shock of his attack brought brief chaos to the customers. Beer glasses slopped, men and women jumped, Chris wheeled round with her eyes wide — and then stared at the two men slowly crumpling at the batwings, red staining their shirts. Both of them were big, dusty, and had apparently travelled a distance.

'What the devil goes on here?' M'Cloud demanded, in the brief silence. 'Who are those mugs, Fletcher?'

'Two guys who followed me frum Oklahoma. I thought I'd ditched them — Reckon I have now, anyways. They're law officers, both uv 'em, spite of their phony saddletramp disguise.'

M'Cloud began to walk towards them but Fletcher's voice stopped him.

'Hold it, M'Cloud.' He began striding between the tables. 'These mugs are my special prize. I'll bury 'em myself . . .'

He stopped when he reached them, turning them over with his boot and surveying their blood-smeared chests.

'You'd better get a look-out on that Oklahoma trail, M'Cloud,' he said, glancing up. 'These law officers would never have got through if you'd had a man there — And while I'm about it you can, all of you, take this as a lesson. I know how to shoot — an' I will if I ever have cause.'

He returned his guns to his holsters, then seizing the men each by a shirt collar he dragged them through the batwings and outside. In a moment he reappeared and looked at the still astonished assembly.

'Be seeing you,' he said. 'I'm burying these mugs off trail somewheres and then going to Ma Grimshaw's — and hurry up gettin' a man on that Oklahoma trail, M'Cloud.'

M'Cloud blinked for a moment and then returned slowly to the bar. He found Ace there, looking at him quizzically. Just behind him Clint Barcliff was scratching the back of his neck.

'Makes yuh begin to wonder who *is* boss around here,' Clint said.

'*I* am!' M'Cloud roared. 'And don't yuh ever forget it. Tip Lacey off to do the Oklahoma trail look-out, will yuh?'

Clint nodded and turned away to obey the order. Ace finished his drink and then gave a grim smile.

'With Fletcher wantin' a cut as well in everythin' yuh do, boss, yuh goin' to find it extra hard t'keep things to yuhself.'

'Blow!' M'Cloud gave him sour look. 'Yo're givin' me a belly ache!'

Ace moved and somehow his silence seemed more eloquent than words. For a long time M'Cloud stood musing and drinking by turns, then it occurred to him that Chris was at his side and that Prentiss was seeing the last of the customers off the premises.

'I've done all I can for now, Vince,' Chris said. 'I might as well be going.'

'Yeah — OK,' he assented moodily.

Chris searched his big, craggy face for a moment. 'I still think I might have been mistaken in you,' she said slowly.

'I said yuh'd find that out.' Vince glanced at her and then away again, his mind clearly wrestling with other issues. 'I s'pose yuh'll come tomorrer night, properly dolled up?'

'Uh-huh. And I'd like my gun back, please.'

'Oh, sure — Sorry.' M'Cloud dragged it from his hip pocket and handed it over. As she took it, Chris reflected how easy it would be for her to fire it straight into M'Cloud's heart and finish the job once and for all. But, surrounded by men and women who would be witnesses, at the mercy of the many gunmen who had come over to M'Cloud's banner? No: she wouldn't stand a chance. The thing to do was to find that cache of hidden gold and then lay plans to get the authorities. The gold was the real *proof* — without it, nothing else counted.

'I sometimes think,' Chris said, as she considered the gun, 'that I've missed quite a deal out of life, Vince. Men, for instance. I never gave them a thought when dad was alive . . . And hard liquor. I always thought it was sinful to drink it 'til I tried it.'

M'Cloud grinned. 'Growing up nicely, ain't you?' he asked. 'Guess I'll have t'improve yuh education as time goes on . . . Anyways, see yuh tomorrer.'

Chris nodded, realizing he was not in a tractable mood. She left him meditating and went to fetch her mackinaw from the dressing-room.

4

After the daily visit of the doctor to see Larry — who was convalescing quite satisfactorily — Chris set off the following morning on a lone search. It would cut down her activities a great deal if she could only find some clue as to where that stage gold had been hidden. At least there was no harm in looking, under the pretext of taking a morning ride. So she rode out casually under the blazing sun to where the trail from Topeka to Dodge City made its closest approach to the Arrow's Flight territory. Certainly she was working on a blind chance, because she had not the remotest idea where the stage had been held up, and even less idea where the gold had been put.

By noon she was no nearer finding anything. She dismounted from her pinto and settled down in the shade of a rock to eat the lunch she had brought with her. Lost in her own thoughts, it came as a shock to her when she realized a man was watching her from nearby, his thumbs hooked on his gun belts. With a sudden feminine instinct she lowered her upraised knees on which her lunch was perched.

'Why the gymnastics?' Abe Fletcher asked, ambling forward. 'Or mebbe you forgot you're wearing riding pants?'

Chris sat looking up at him — his saturnine face, the hard set of his mouth, the bleak grey eyes. She felt afraid, but did not dare to show it. Remembering his onslaught in the saloon the previous evening, she was pretty sure he'd stop at nothing if he once guessed she was scared.

'How did you get here?' she demanded. 'Can't I even take a morning ride without you following me?'

'I didn't follow you, Chris.' He had come to within a foot of her, and now paused. 'I'm ridin' around, too —

looking for gold. I make no secret of it. If I could find it I'd take the lot and vamoose. I've no mistaken notions about loyalty. In this region it's every guy for himself. If I don't take the gold first, M'Cloud will. It's as simple as that. He sure won't share it with me or any other man — not unless he's loco.'

Chris was not quite sure what she ought to do next — whether to run for it, snatch out her gun and brandish it, or — As it happened, Abe Fletcher settled the issue for her. He plumped down beside her and cuffed up his sombrero on to his wide forehead. He looked less sinister with his full face in view.

'Don't worry,' he said drily. 'I don't aim t' hurt you, Chris. I'd be a mug to hurt what I like — How's about a sandwich? I didn't bring any food, and that old dame Ma Grimshaw is one helluva chiseller.'

Mechanically Chris handed over the sandwiches. He took one and munched it thoughtfully. All the time he kept his hard eyes upon her, until at last she could stand it no longer.

'Why on earth do you keep *looking* at me?' she demanded. 'Or did you never see a girl before?'

'Seen plenty, but none like you. I'm trying to weigh up what a girl like you wants trucking around with a no-good like M'Cloud. Don't make sense.'

'You should talk! You're a self-admitted killer and a thief — and I saw with my own eyes what happened last night — and then you start slanging M'Cloud.'

'That don't answer the question. What do you want playin' around with him? He ain't got anything I haven't. Probably not as much.'

'Meaning what?' Chris demanded.

'Depends. If you're just lookin' for a man who'd make a good husband and blast hell out of guys you don't like, I'm the man.'

Chris opened her mouth and then shut it again. Fletcher raised the top leaf of his sandwich and inspected the beef.

'Good stuff,' he said. 'From your own beef herds?'

'Yes. And I think the sooner you realize how things stand in regard to me, the better. I'm working for M'Cloud because I like it — and I trust him more than I do you. That settle matters for you?'

'No. I think you're a liar.'

'Why, you — '

'Because nobody *could* trust M'Cloud. He's got 'outlaw' stamped all over his ugly map. You've another reason for working beside him and I'm just plumb curious t' know what it is.'

'It's my own business, anyways,' Chris said, getting to her feet in sudden purpose. 'Apart from being impudent, Mr Fletcher, you're inquisitive as well — and I don't like it.'

He grinned for the first time and stood up beside her.

'No sense in being backward,' he raid casually. 'If you're headin' back to your spread. I'll keep you company.'

Chris's only response was an angry

look. Her own plans for spending the remainder of the afternoon in searching were now blown sky high. She went across to her horse and his footsteps followed behind her. She swung to the saddle and rode away without even so much as a backward glance at him — but she had not been long on the trail for home when he caught up with her.

'What's your objection to me?' he asked, puzzled, his eyes narrowed against the glare of the sunlight.

Chris did not reply for a moment. The wind was threshing back the auburn hair from her face, making her silk shirt cling against her well moulded body.

'You admit you're a killer and then shoot two men down in cold blood — and ask me my objection to you!' She gave a contemptuous glance. 'Pretty clear, isn't it? What did you do with those two law officers, anyway?'

'Buried 'em. It's mighty nice t' do things in safety like that. Nobody can chase after me 'cos the trail's watched from here on. I guess M'Cloud has this territory nicely closed up.'

'And us inside it! I'm going to break through the barrier before I'm finished.'

'Which is why you're clinging to M'Cloud, mebbe?'

Chris made no answer. She was having a struggle to decide whether she thoroughly detested or secretly liked this man with the hard grey eyes and unready smile. Somehow, in spite of his iron exterior, he seemed to have something deep inside him which was genuine — But the fact remained he had killed two men within sight of everybody. Chris asked herself if she was entitled to judge him on this point. Had she not herself shot down the murderer of her father? Perhaps a gun was the only answer in this lawless territory, anyway . . .

Fletcher did not make any more comments on the journey back. When the yard of the Forked-J had been reached he swung down easily from the saddle and held up his powerful hands to help Chris. She gave him a stony look.

'I've been getting off a horse — and on one — since I was six years old, Mr Fletcher,' she told him. 'I don't need your help.'

'Mebbe it's the gentleman in me,' he replied drily. 'You wouldn't want to kill that instinct, would you?'

She frowned, trying to puzzle him out, then she drew one leg over the saddle. The next moment his hands were beneath her armpits and lifting her down gently. He held her for a moment, looking into her violet eyes.

'Like I said, you've got looks, Chris . . . ' and he kissed her full on the mouth. Instantly she pulled free of his grip and hit him hard across the face. As on the previous occasion he did not even flinch.

'Do nothing but take advantage, do you?' Chris demanded hotly.

'If I like a thing, I show it.' he replied, shrugging. 'Anyway, I'm not apologizing. You're a nice girl, and I'll see more of you later . . . 'Bye for now. When you know me better mebbe you'll tell me why you hang close to that louse M'Cloud.'

She stared after him in surprise, but he did not once look back. Remounting his horse, he rode out of the yard and was soon lost to sight along the trail to Arrow's Flight . . .

For the remainder of the afternoon and early evening Chris thought a lot about him — more in a puzzled vein than anything else, then at last she dismissed him from her mind as she remembered but one thing. He was a murderer.

Towards eight o'clock she arrived as usual at the Yellow Nugget, this time in her evening gown, and full of the determination to try and get M'Cloud to talk. In fact, she had all kinds of elaborate plans. She would get him intoxicated, if that were possible, lure him on by every feminine trick she knew, until she learned where that gold was. Then she would take a chance and try to get help from Dodge City. Not Topeka: the flat country made a rider too much of a target: but with the hilly district between her and Dodge City she might get away with it.

But things did not work out. M'Cloud did little but give her a brief greeting, and the rest of the evening he was not even in the saloon, nor were most of his men. Only a few were around to shoot down any trouble: the rest had vanished. In truth, all of them were in M'Cloud's private office, including Abe Fletcher, deep in plans for the hold-up of the stage coach the following day.

So beyond a goodnight when the evening's business was over, Chris did not advance her own schemes one jot. It annoyed her. Every time she missed an opportunity she felt that M'Cloud, got a firmer grip on the unresisting population. However, she meant to try again — probably the following night, if chances were at all improved.

M'Cloud, for his part, hardly gave a

thought to her. He had too many other matters on his mind. By mid-morning on the following day he, Ace, and Abe Fletcher were on their way to make the hold-up, their position selected — a point two miles east of the location of their previous attack. They reached it in the early afternoon, tied their horses in the cover of giant rocks at the trail side, and then sat themselves down in the dust to wait.

'There may be trouble this time,' M'Cloud said, watching the as yet empty trail. 'Those jiggers'll be wary after the last lot and may open up on sight. Only answer to that one is shoot first.'

'Which is crazy,' Fletcher said.

M'Cloud spat. 'Why is it? That's what we agreed on — '

'Y'mean you did, M'Cloud. I'm saying what I think. Like as not there'll be passengers on that stage — an' if you shoot down the rider an' his ramrod how d'you figger those folk is going to get to Dodge City? Only two answers

97

— either one of us drives 'em there, which is impossible, or we take them amongst our mob, where they'll be nothing but trouble. Get wise to yourself, M'Cloud. This game's risky enough without adding trouble.'

'The guy's right,' Ace said, thinking.

'You *would* think so,' M'Cloud sneered. 'All right then, how do we handle it if we don't shoot first? Tell me that!'

Fletcher shrugged. 'Simple enough. Let the coach go past and then follow it with our horses and hold it up from the rear. The driver and his ramrod won't be expecting that. We'll have them covered before they can turn around and shoot.'

Ace's eyes opened wider. 'Say, the guy's got brains, boss!'

M'Cloud muttered something, but he nodded just the same.

'OK, Fletcher. Mebbe yo're right. We'd better get on our horses ready.'

The animals were unreined, and mounted; then, after another long wait, there came the unmistakable jingling of harness and the growing thunder of wheels on the sun-baked earth. At last the stage came into view in the distance and just as M'Cloud had anticipated, the two men on the box seat had their guns ready. The driver was holding the reins with one hand and a revolver in the other, his head glancing from side to side. The ramrod for his part had a rifle on his knees, ready for instant action.

The stage swept past and M'Cloud gave a grin. Then he pulled up his 'kerchief and spurred his horse out of concealment. At top speed he went racing away after the stage, with the masked Ace and Fletcher following behind. Warning shots and then orders brought the stage to a halt. Obviously furious with themselves at the assault from the rear, the driver and ramrod raised their hands.

'You sure got some nerve, you mugs.' the driver snapped. 'The Dodge City Feds, are already lookin' fur yuh. When they know 'bout this lot they'll redouble their efforts. Yuh just can't git away with it.'

'Shut up,' M'Cloud retorted. 'An' kick down that box.'

That which followed was practically a repetition of the previous robbery. Whilst M'Cloud blew open the box and satisfied himself gold was inside it, Fletcher took a look at the stage's passengers. Two men and a woman, all three of them sitting tight and hoping for the best. Nothing there that mattered. Ace kept a little to the rear, his greedy eyes on the gold ingots.

'OK, on your way,' M'Cloud said finally. 'Tell 'em what yuh like in Dodge City; they sure won't ever find us.'

The stage began to move, gathered speed, and at last lost itself in the clouds of dust along the trail. Fletcher and Ace dismounted from their horses, looked at the gold — then at M'Cloud.

'Where's the hiding place?' Fletcher asked.

M'Cloud rose up from the case, then

suddenly brought up his right-hand gun.

'I'm not goin' through all this agin,' he said briefly. 'Ace asked me that last time — and the answer's the same. I'm not sayin' where I hide it 'til I'm good and ready. The both uv yuh can hit it back to Arrow's Flight right now.'

'See what I mean?' Ace asked drily. 'Whole thing smells of a double-cross to me.'

'Mebbe. Mebbe not.' Fletcher mused for a moment. 'I don't think you'd try and pull anything when the share-out comes, M'Cloud, because you know the rest of us'd get you if you did, no matter where you went. OK, play the game your way right now — since you've got your gun out first. When it comes to the cut we'll all have something to say.'

He turned to his horse, mounted it, then waited for Ace to do likewise. Together they began riding away, leaving M'Cloud with the box at his feet.

'You crazy?' Ace asked, as Fletcher rode beside him. 'We might have had the drop on him then.'

'I doubt it, with his rod on us. But s'pposin' we'd have killed him. What'd be the use of it? Five thousand in gold is pretty good, but what about the other ten thousand he's hidden? If we'd shot him we'd never have found it. We want it all, Ace, or nothing — and we'll make him tell us where it is before we're through.'

'Yuh don't know Vince M'Cloud,' Ace said grimly.

'Mebbe not — but I *do* know Abe Fletcher. I'll make him talk before I'm through. In the meantime, let him go on buryin' the stuff and stealin' it. Be all the more for us when we're ready to make a dash for it.'

'Y' mean just vou an' me?'

'Sure thing. We're pardners, ain't we? Why should we include the rest of the bunch who don't take any risks?'

★ ★ ★

Chris Dawlish heard all about the second stage robbery as she came into town that evening on the buckboard. She first heard punchers discussing it on the boardwalk as she lashed the horses' reins to the tie-rack, and it seemed to be the only topic of conversation in the Yellow Nugget. In fact, the telegraphist in touch with Dodge City was having another field day. The authorities had doubled their reward offer for the robbers, and the sheriff of Arrow's Flight, in common with other sheriffs, had been tipped off to keep a look-out for the bandits — which fact amused Clint Barcliff not a little.

That M'Cloud and his boys had done the job was an open secret. Having the whole town's population just where he wanted it, M'Cloud made no pretence of hiding his actions any longer. To Chris it meant that it was time she got some action. There must be two lots of gold now, their exact location worth the time of any law officer to come and investigate.

Throughout the evening, following her usual routine with the customers, she watched her chance. Abe Fletcher passed a few words with her, but left it at that, since M'Cloud's eye was upon him. M'Cloud himself did not seem likely to make any moves, so Chris used her own strategy and fainted away gracefully in the middle of the floor. Just as she had expected, first Fletcher and then M'Cloud rushed to her assistance. She saw them through her eyelashes.

'This is my job,' M'Cloud said curtly, elbowing Fletcher out of the way. 'I'll fix her up — Have some brandy sent to my private office.'

Chris found herself swept up and then carried in M'Cloud's powerful arms through the back passage and into the rear office. M'Cloud kicked the door shut and then laid her on the couch, rubbing at her hands steadily. Presently the brandy was brought. Chris drank some, spluttered and coughed over its sting, and stirred realistically back to life.

'I — I do believe I passed out,' she said slowly, as M'Cloud stooped over her.

'Sure yuh did, kid. Mebbe the work's too much for yuh. The stink uv beer and tobacco fumes — Not so hot fur an open-air gal like you.'

'That must be it,' she admitted, a hand to her forehead. 'Anyway, maybe it's given us a chance to be together for once. You don't have to go, do you?'

'Not if you don't want me to.' M'Cloud gave a grin and pulled up a chair to the sofa. He straddled it and considered her. 'What's on your mind, Chris?'

'Oh . . . just that I've been doing a lot of thinking lately. You once said I might get to know you better one day. Well, I think I do right now.'

'Yeah?' There was vague suspicion in his blue eyes.

'I'm lonely,' Chris said, lowering her hand and giving him a frank look. 'Now dad's gone, there's just nothing. I even enjoy coming here at night now, just for the company. I still don't like the work. When I think how lonely the future's going to be I get just a little scared.'

'A man could cure it,' M'Cloud said.

'That's just what I was thinking.'

There was silence for a moment. Chris could feel her heart bumping painfully at the long chance she was taking, but the fear she felt did not show in her expression. She raised herself up on one elbow from the couch.

'I'll tell you, how I look at it, Vince. You say you like me — '

'Sure I do. I think yore the nicest gal I ever saw.'

'Well, at first I detested you. I detested you even more for your threats — and when my dad was murdered I thought I ought to kill you. Now I know it was mainly his — his own fault, not yours. As for you — Well, I shot a man down myself, so I can sort of feel the way you do when you're protecting yourself. Add to that the fact that you're the most important man hereabouts, and that I'm one of the best looking girls — so you say — and it seems to amount to something.'

'Say, this begins to make sense!' M'Cloud exclaimed, jumping up and pushing the chair away. 'It even sounds as though yuh figger we oughta run double harness.'

'That's it,' Chris admitted quietly. 'At least I'd be safe with you back of me and I sort of understand you now.'

M'Cloud grinned, stooped, and put his great hands behind her bare shoulders. She had to submit to his kisses and look happy when he had finished.

'We're goin' right out to tell the folks!' he said at last, lifting her bodily from the couch and then setting her on her feet. 'Vince M'Cloud and his wife ter be. That'll sure sock that coyote Abe Fletcher in the eye. I think he's had a fancy fur you himself.'

'Him?' Chris gave a contemptuous

laugh. 'I don't like him. He's cold — snake-like. I wouldn't trust him across the street. But look, Vince' — she caught his arm — 'surely we can celebrate on our own first? I'm not up to going amongst everybody with all that excitement right now. I'm still wobbly.'

'Sure, sure. I'm fergittin'. We'll drink our health in here. Best stuff in the house. You sit here . . . '

He settled her at the table and then hurried to the door. Opening it, he bawled into the passage:

'Hey, Baldy! There's some champagne somewheres there — bring it. The lot! It's important.'

Grinning, M'Cloud came back into the room. Chris smiled at him, realizing her legs were quivering uncomfortably. The next half hour was going to be the toughest she had ever endured.

In a moment or two Baldy had arrived. He put the three champagne bottles on the table, glasses beside them, and then beat a retreat as M'Cloud jerked his head at him.

Getting up, M'Cloud went to the door and locked it, then returned to the table. The champagne cork flew out of the bottle neck with the explosion of a revolver shot.

'Yuh've sure got sense, Chris,' M'Cloud said, handing over the glass of bubbling liquid. 'Here — take this. Make yuh feel on top uv the world.'

Chris took a sip, jerked half the contents over her shoulder whilst M'Cloud was preoccupied with filling his own glass, and then met his gaze across the table.

'Ter you an' me,' he said, and drank the champagne off at one gulp.

That was the beginning. He refilled the glasses, and talked faster as he did so. Chris was compelled to drink some of the champagne, but not enough to fuddle her senses. M'Cloud, as she had hoped, had the fixed determination to empty all the bottles. And, hardened drinker though he was, the champagne at last began to have a real effect. His movements became less steady, his terms of endearment more amorous. Chris watched him intently.

'Wass the matter?' he asked at last, getting up and holding on to the table edge. 'We're s'posed t'be engaged ain't we? No ring yet — but there *will* be! Yes, *sir!* What 'bout the kisses? I ain't seen many so fur. C'm here an' kiss Vince . . . '

He reached out his band and grabbed her arm tightly, half dragging her out of her chair. She resisted for a moment, and then let him have his way. She finished up on his knees as he sat down again at the table.

'Sure you rate a kiss, Vince,' she murmured, and gave him one. Then she coiled her arm round the back of his neck and began to play gently with his untidy hair. 'But getting engaged like we have means more things than just a kiss . . . We ought not to have any secrets from each other.'

'Yeah, yeah, dead right,' he agreed emphatically. 'Bes' way t'start. No secrets!'

'I haven't any that I know of,' Chris mused. 'I've openly admitted I was wrong about you, and I think that's all there is — but with you it's different. I want to know how much the man I'm going to marry is worth.'

'Thousands,' he replied, grinning, then swallowing more of the now flat champagne. 'Thousands, Chris. Yuh ain't got no need t'worry.'

'But I *do* worry. Those thousands you're talking about are hidden, aren't they?'

'Sure they are. Good an' deep.'

'Well then — suppose somebody else finds them first? We won't have much money between us, will we? Only what I've got from the ranch — But that wouldn't suit you. You want to keep *me*, not me keep you.'

M'Cloud got up slowly, setting her on her feet. Then he caught her shoulders and held on to them tightly. She could feel him swaying as he spoke.

'Lissen, Chris, that gold is where nobody c'n find it. An' it'll stop that way. All fur you an' me — '

'Then I ought to know where it is so I can keep an eye on it when you can't.'

Chris waited anxiously as M'Cloud considered this. He took his hands from her shoulders and promptly sat down. He rubbed his face and forehead slowly.

'Mebbe yore right,' he muttered. 'I reckon if a guy can't trust the gal he's goin' ter marry he might as well not waste his time.'

'You can trust me, Vince,' Chris smiled, her arms about his neck as she kissed him again. 'Here — have some more champagne.'

She emptied the dregs from the three bottles and made him drink up. Since he was already confused and hardly able to sit up straight the extra champagne made little difference. For a moment or two he seemed to have gone to sleep, then he begun fumbling in his jacket and produced a piece of paper. With a pencil he began to draw a diagram.

'I wouldn't do this fur — hup! — any

gal I don't trust,' he muttered, closing one eye so he could focus a little more comfortably. 'Yuh've taken a chance on me, kid, so I guess I'm taking one on you — See, here's where the gold is. This is the trail an' here is where th' first lot uv stuff is buried. Right — hup! — by a marked rock. Can't mistake it. The other lot's further away . . . '

He yawned as he came to the finish of his drawing, then his head began to droop. Very cautiously Chris withdrew the sketch from under his big hand, folded it, and slipped it into her dress. By the time she had reached the door he was snoring heavily. She unlocked it and hurried out into the corridor. In five more minutes she was in her buckboard and, her dustcoat muffling her to the ears, she began riding through the night.

5

It was well after midnight when Chris reached the Topeka — Dodge City trail, a trip which she made in record time since she knew every inch of the route from Arrow's Flight. Here she drew the snorting team to a halt, studied the sketch in the brilliant moonlight, then jumped down and began to look about her. As far as she could judge she was not very far from the rock out cropping the sketch indicated . . . So she began searching.

It took her thirty minutes to locate the right position and once she had done this she began burrowing in the sandy soil until her hands struck on something metallic. Quickly she cleared away the last traces of soil and pulled hard on the lid of the buried box. In the moonlight, the ingots glimmered dully.

'Just what the doctor ordered, eh Chris?'

Her heart racing, she looked round quickly, from her crouched position. Only a couple of feet behind her stood Abe Fletcher, clearly visible in the moonlight. He had made no noise approaching in the loose sandy soil. A dim shape in the distance was probably his horse.

'OK, I'm not going to shoot,' he said, spreading his hands. 'I haven't even got my gun out.'

Chris got up slowly, staring at him. She could see every one of her plans crumbling right before her eyes.

'How did you get here?' she demanded.

'Followed you, I guess. I heard everything M'Cloud said in his private office.'

'But — but how *could* you have done?'

'Simple enough. I saw you and M'Cloud head for his private office, and afterwards he yelled for champagne. You don't want stuff like that without there being a celebration — so, since I reckon I have as much right

115

t'you as M'Cloud, I had a listen outside the office door. Easy to do in that deserted passage. I heard all he had to say and gathered you'd discovered where he'd hidden the gold. So I followed you at a safe distance . . . Satisfied?'

'And now you've found it — thanks to me — you mean to run awavy with it, I suppose?'

Fletcher came closer. 'There's another lot somewheres, and I want that, too. You've got a sketch plan, haven't you?'

'Yes. And I'm sticking to it! Listen to me, Mr Fletcher, I'm only interested in this gold because I want it as proof. I want to bring a marshal here if I can and show him this loot, then let M'Cloud explain it away — if he can. And I mean to defend my discovery, too, after all I've been through to get at it!'

Abruptly Chris's gun gleamed in her hand. Fletcher looked at it, then back to her face.

'So that's been the reason for you

sticking so close to M'Cloud. To track down this gold?'

'Right! Don't forget, he murdered my father — and I've been through purgatory making love to M'Cloud. I can't bring the law to deal with him without some visible proof of his dirty work. So, I had to find out where he buried the stuff.'

'That's what I wanted to know, too,' Fletcher said.

'So you can run away with it!'

'No — so's I can arrest him.'

Chris gave a start. 'So you can *what?*' she gasped.

'Sorry if I've seemed unpleasant,' Fletcher said, his hard voice changing curiously so that it became pleasantly cultured. 'I've had one tough role to play, Miss Dawlish — just the same as you have. We've both been after the same thing apparently — proof.'

'But — but who *are* you?' Chris demanded, her gun wavering.

Fletcher came forward, ignoring her weapon. From his shirt pocket he took a badge and held it out in his palm.

'I'm Dick Milford, a marshal from Dodge City,' he explained. 'I was sent over here by the authorities after the first stage hold-up. Since I could never have gotten into Arrow's Flight in the ordinary way I became a tough killer on the run . . . '

'But you said you shot a look-out of M'Cloud's!'

'He wasn't shot — just knocked out. I came with four of my own men, and between us we took care of that guy. Two of my boys took him back to Dodge and jail. The other two, primed in advance, were the ones I apparently murdered in the saloon.'

'You — you mean — '

'Just a build-up,' Dick Milford smiled. 'They did their job well with cochineal for blood. Don't forget, I wouldn't allow anybody to examine them. Instead of me burying them they just took up quarters near the town, waiting for new orders from me. As for that reward notice concerning me: it was a fake. I had to convince M'Cloud I was a genuine outlaw. What puzzled me was *your* angle in the whole thing, which is why I tried to question you by yourself. Since you've openly admitted what you are driving at there's no point in my holding out on you. I'm sorry for anything I may have said that sounded offensive: I had to stay in character.'

Chris smiled, put her gun away, then held out her hand.

'All forgiven, Mr Milford. I might as well admit there were times when you didn't quite convince me . . . But to get back to the point, what happens now? It won't take long to discover where the later cache is hidden: what then?'

'I'll remove the cases to a place of my own choosing and head straight away for Dodge City to bring back a posse who can arrest M'Cloud and clean up the rest of his bunch. I can get past the look-out easily enough. I could have done so long ago, only, like you, I wanted some tangible evidence of M'Cloud's misdemeanours before doing so. Now I have it — '

'Hope it does yuh some good, feller!' a voice barked from amidst the nearby rocks. 'Git yuh hands up, the both uv yuh!'

Instantly Dick Milford swung round, his gun whisking from its holster. He fired twice at the dim rockery, but evidently without effect, for the voice spoke again.

'Better not waste slugs in this uncertain light, Marshal. Yuh can't see me amidst the rockery, but I can see you — and the dame — against the sand. Come this way — and keep yuh hands up.'

Milford slowly raised his arms and gave the girl a grim glance in the moonlight.

'Better do as he says, Miss Dawlish. He's got a bead on us all right.'

They began walking forward until they were both commanded to halt; then the gunman came slowly into view.

He took their weapons from them and gave a dry chuckle. The moonlight revealed him as Ace.

'This is sure goin' ter hand the boss a laugh,' he commented. 'The tough guy killer turns out to be a marshal! Whadda ya know!'

'Naturally, you followed me?' Milford asked curtly.

'Nope; I followed the gal here. The boss called me and sed he figgered that mebbe he'd talked too much when he had too much firewater in his belly — so just in case the dame got up to something he told me where she'd probably gone. Out I came to see, and I caught sight of her in the distance. All I had t'do was follow her. I was just about set to deal with her when you turned up. Mighty good job I kept hidden an' heard all yuh had to say. I sure learned plenty.'

'I never saw you whilst I followed Miss Dawlish,' Millord said, puzzled.

'Not likely yuh would. I took the back trail. Knowin' where she wus headed I'd no need ter keep her in sight.'

There was silence for a moment. Keeping his guns trained, the gunman walked back to where the box of ingots lay. He kicked the lid shut with his foot, then with the same foot scraped the sandy soil back into place.

'Might be useful ter me later t'know where this stuff is,' he said. 'But there's also the other one. Yuh've got a sketch of it, Chris. I want it!'

'Try getting it!' she retorted.

'OK — if that's the way yuh want it . . . ' Ace came forward and dug his free hand into her shirt pockets. He found the paper in the right hand one and pulled it out.

'Much obliged,' he said drily. 'Now both uv yuh git on yuh horses. An' don't try anythin', neither. The boss is goin' t'enjoy this quite a lot.'

Chris and Milford exchanged looks, but they had no other course than to obey. When they were in the saddles Ace made doubly sure of them by one-handedly roping their wrists to the saddles at the rear; then he went for his own horse and mounted it.

'Get goin',' he snapped, and stayed in the rear of the two as they nudged their mounts forward.

★　★　★

Though the Yellow Nugget was closed for business when the trio returned to town, M'Cloud himself was still there, in his private office, waiting for whatever information Ace might bring back. He stood staring in amazed fury as both Chris and 'Abe Fletcher' were brought before him.

'What gives?' he asked, swinging on Ace. 'What are these two doin' together?'

'Just like I told yuh, boss,' Ace replied, shrugging. 'This guy here who yuh made such a play fur is a marshal — Milford, of the Dodge City authorities.'

'Marshal?' M'Cloud eyed Milford in

rising fury. He was no longer drunk, but the after effects had not improved his temper.

'*Marshal?*'

'Yeah. Take a look at this. I just took it off'n him.'

Ace held out the badge which he had removed from Milford's shirt just before entering the saloon. M'Cloud studied it in the lamplight, then he looked up with a hard grin.

'Congratulations, feller. Yuh certainly had me fooled!'

'It wasn't difficult,' Milford answered shrugging.

'No? Didn't do yuh much good, did it? I guess you fooled me too, Chris,' M'Cloud continued. 'I figgered yuh wus on the level. Now I know better. Serves me right: I shouldn't trust wimmin.' He jammed the badge back in Milford's shirt pocket.

'She found the gold, boss,' Ace added. 'The ten thousand dollar lot.'

'Yeah?' M'Cloud's expression changed. 'Which means you know where it is, huh? Well yuh won't fur long: I'll fix that. Meantime I reckon there's a necktie party due to yuh, Marshal.'

'On what grounds?' Milford asked grimly. 'I didn't murder anybody.'

'No? What about them two men yuh shot down 'cos yuh sed they wus chasing yuh?'

'They're still alive. They were sidekicks of mine.'

M'Cloud grinned. 'Can yuh prove it? I reckon not, 'cos I won't give yuh the chance. So if yuh swing for that the populace can't say I don't know how to dispense justice.'

'You're getting in too deep, M'Cloud,' Milford warned him. 'I'm no ordinary man, remember: I'm a marshal. The whole bunch of law men will be round your neck if you touch me.'

'They may be round me neck anyways, so I'll at least git the satisfaction uv givin' yuh a farewell party. An' that'll be at dawn brother. Meantime, tie him to that chair, Ace.'

Since he was still covered by guns

Milford had no chance to resist. He submitted passively to being fastened securely to one of the big office chairs, his hands tied behind him.

'What about the dame?' Ace demanded. 'I guess she's a bigger double-crosser than the marshal. Pretendin' ter love yuh — wantin' t'marry yuh. She oughta be in the neck-tie party, too.'

'Shut up, you; I'll handle this.' M'Cloud went over to her and she backed away a few paces. 'I've no intention uv hangin' yuh, Chris, 'cos I couldn't bear ter see a neck as purty as yours stretched too fur. What I *am* goin' ter do is hold yuh to yuh promise. Yore goin' ter marry me, whether yuh like it or not. Yuh don't return to that ranch o' yours: yuh don't go any place, 'cept I'm with yuh. Got that?'

She did not answer. Her eyes wide and fixed, she kept on staring at him. Finally she had backed to a chair by the wall, and seated herself, watching him.

'Fine pair uv conspirators,' he said cynically, glancing from one to the other. 'An' don't you think, Ace, yuh pullin' any fast ones about that gold uv mine . . . Which reminds me, I remember drawin' a sketch for yuh. Chris. Where is it?'

Ace glanced at the girl sharply and cocked his gun. The barrel pointed straight at her face. M'Cloud saw the action and turned slowly.

'So that's it,' he breathed. 'Yuh took the sketch frum her and mean ter blow her brains out if she dare say so. Why you cheap, dirty side-winder — '

'Hold it, boss,' Ace warned, his gun ready. 'Sure as hell I'll blast yuh if yuh take another step. I've wanted ter have the drop on yuh fur long enough, and now I've got it. Yore at the wrong end of the hardware and I know where all that gold is. You don't expect me ter pass up a chance like that, do yuh?'

M'Cloud stood motionless, his eyes slitted, Ace crouched against the wall with his gun steady. Chris remained where she was, watching intently, but her dangling hand was straying to the metal bin nearby which served as a waste-paper basket. She had one thought at the moment: to be at the mercy of M'Cloud was better than to be at the mercy of Ace. Ace was a sadistic killer: M'Cloud was a thug with some gleams of decency in his toughness. Therein lay a vital difference —

And abruptly the paper basket sailed through the air. It did no damage, but it was a complete distraction for Ace. He looked up sharply as the tin bin sailed towards him — then M'Cloud's fist crashed into his face with stunning impact, slamming his head hard against the wall. The revolver was whipped out of his hand and he began reeling before a battering onslaught of mighty punches. Gasping with pain he sank to his knees, and he never rose from them. The revolver began exploding with relentless violence, and M'Cloud didn't stop until the hammer clicked futilely. His face black with rage, he tossed the useless weapon on the desk and stared down for a moment on the silent Ace.

'Dirty, twistin' coyote,' he muttered; then he relaxed a little and turned to where Chris was sitting. 'Thanks, Chris, fur doin' that. I shouldn't ha' thought you'd have figgered I wus worth savin'.'

'You're not,' Chris answered coldly. 'But of two dirty crooks I prefer you.'

'Always kiddin',' M'Cloud said drily; then he hauled up the corpse of Ace and dragged it into a corner. He came back into the centre of the office, dusting his hands. 'I'll have the boys ditch that later,' he said. 'Right now we're alone here, with nothin' t'do but wait for the dawn. Then, brother, you're goin' t'start swingin'.'

M'Cloud looked up sharply for a moment, towards the window. It was partly open at the top. He fancied he had heard some slight sound — nor was he alone in his belief. Chris and Milford had also heard it, but it could have been the wind.

Yanking out his own gun M'Cloud strode forward, flung up the bottom sash, and looked outside. There was nothing visible in the little back alleyway which the window overlooked.

'Must be gettin' jittery,' M'Cloud muttered, slamming the window down again; then he went over to his swivel chair and threw himself into it. Taking a bottle of whiskey from the lower drawer, he poured out a drink and handed it to Chris.

'No thanks,' she said, and eyed him fixedly.

'Off the hard liquor again? Too bad! Sorry I can't accommodate you, Marshal. I make it a principle never ter help marshals any if I c'n avoid it.'

Milford made no comment. He just sat watching either M'Cloud or Chris.

'We're stuck here 'til dawn,' M'Cloud said, finishing his drink. 'So just make yuhselves comfortable. I've had some sleep, so I don't need any. But you look all in, Chris.'

She pretty nearly was, but not for anything would she have admitted it. As it happened, however, Nature herself took the job in hand and forced her to sleep. When she awakened again she was still in the chair, stiff and cramped, her head lolling back against the wall. Grey light was showing against the office window. M'Cloud was in his swivel chair, his feet on the desk, his revolver ready in his hand. He was half asleep and half awake, but he stirred as the girl moved. Milford was still awake nearly dead with cramp, his face set in grim lines.

'One sure test of a woman, Chris,' M'Cloud said, getting up and stretching his arms. 'If she looks as purty in a morning when she just wakes up as she does the rest uv the time, she's got somethin'. An' you sure have! How's about some breakfast before the neck-tie party?'

'You can stand there and ask me that?' she cried. 'What do you take me for?'

M'Cloud shrugged, then he went about the business of untying Milford's ropes. The marshal stretched his aching limbs and rubbed them for a moment or two; then he got to his feet.

'Start walking,' M'Cloud ordered, his gun ready. 'I aim to make yuh walk up the main street to where the sycamore tree is: that's where all the hangings is done in this territory, I'm told. As we go I c'n shout to the populace what's comin'. I guess we'll have a nice little party around us by the time we finish the walk. All I haveta do then is explain that yuh bein' hanged for the murder of them two law officers — an' that'll be that . . . You start moving too, Chris. I don't trust yuh behind me.'

The girl moved, drawing her mackinaw about her shoulders. She looked washed out, tired, utterly incongruous at this hour of the morning with her long evening gown sweeping the dusty floor.

Keeping both her and Milford covered M'Cloud drew back the heavy bolts on the office door and then stepped outside. The moment he did so he gave a gasp as a gun drove hard into his spine.

'Hold it, M'Cloud,' a voice murmured. 'Drop your gun!'

It clattered from M'Cloud's hand to the boardwalk. He tried to angle his head round and caught a glimpse of two men in Stetsons. A look of relief swept Milford's face.

'Good work, boys,' he exclaimed, moving forward, and picking up M'Cloud's gun for his own use. 'I was just about due for a neck-tie party — '

'We knew that, Dick,' one of the men answered. 'Last night when we heard shots from the office we came over to investigate. We heard this louse sayin' what he figgered on doing — so we waited 'til he came out of his office. No use trying to bust in earlier with those bolts on: it'd have given him warning. You're safe enough now, anyways — and you too, Miss Dawlish.'

'Why, I know you two men!' Chris exclaimed suddenly, recognizing them.

'You were 'shot' by Mr Milford in the saloon!'

'Right,' Milford grinned. 'I told you they were camping near the town until I needed them. And keeping a watch on me, too, from the look of things.'

'Sure.' One of them agreed. 'We saw you, Miss Dawlish, and that gorilla come riding back in the small hours — and the shots made us think the worst. Anyways, Dick, what's the next move? Arrest this louse?'

'Just that,' Milford responded, and he moved forward.

At the identical moment M'Cloud, desperate, took a long chance with the gun in his spine and lashed out his fist straight to Milford's jaw. He staggered under the blow and fell backwards through the open doorway of the office. Before he could get on his feet again M'Cloud had snatched Chris to him, an arm about her waist, using her as a shield. Then he began to back along the boardwalk, ignoring her desperate struggles to free herself.

'Take me if y'can!' he shouted, as the men tried helplessly to aim at him. 'If yuh kill me it'll be through her — and that wouldn't be so nice.'

Cursing to himself Milford struggled up, his gun still in his hand. He hurried forward after the retreating M'Cloud, but there was just nothing he could do. Chris was the perfect, if unco-operative shield. Whichever way Milford swung, the girl was swung too.

Then Milford glanced up as other men began to appear in the distance — the early risers, the cattle tenders, the cow-punchers, the farm hands. He gave a desperate glance towards Chris as M'Cloud still moved along with her.

'Better get movin', Dick,' one of his men cried, hurrying to him. 'These other guys may be with M'Cloud. If so, we'll get no place. I reckon Miss Dawlish won't get hurt much: M'Cloud's too gone on her for that — but you'll get a hanging if you're caught. Mebbe all of us will. Better move.'

Milford gave a last look up and

down, and then nodded.

'Mebbe you're right. We'll figure out a way of getting Chris later on. Got your horses handy?'

'Sure thing. Over there by the livery stable.'

'Mine's at the tie rack there. Let's go.'

Milford began moving fast. He unfastened his horse's reins from the rail outside the saloon, swung to the saddle, and then began to gallop out of town as fast as he could go. In a few minutes his two colleagues had caught up with him.

'Where are we making for?' one of them asked.

'The spot where the ten thousand dollar gold consignment is buried,' Milford answered. 'I want that at all costs, and I don't see anything in the way of getting it, either. Once I have that it's proof of M'Cloud's dirty work. After that we find a way to reach Dodge City and get the rest of the boys down here to clean up. We'll make a base in the mountains for the time being.'

'And what happens about the girl?'

Milford's face clouded for a moment. 'I dunno. I'll have to find a way somehow to get her out of M'Cloud's clutches . . . '

He said no more for the moment, but kept on riding hard. It was not long before the sound of drumming hooves to the rear made him glance back. His men looked too, and they exchanged grim looks.

'Looks like M'Cloud has figgered out what you're going to do,' one of the men said. 'We can't make it ahead of them at the rate we're going. We'd better stop an' fight it out.'

Milford looked ahead. The journey to the site of the buried gold was considerable, even yet. Certainly it would not be possible to reach it without being overtaken. To the rear there were a dozen men, moving like the wind, their guns exploding in the air as a warning of their intentions.

'All right, we stop and fight it out,'

Milford said curtly. 'Turn aside. This rockery here'll be good cover.'

He swung round his horse's head and hurtled the animal into the midst of nearby rock spurs. In those few seconds the pursuing horsemen covered a good deal more ground, but for some reason they did not make any particularly violent retaliation to the bullets which shattered in their direction. Two of their number dropped heavily from the saddle, and by that time Milford was realizing the uselessness of fighting further. He and his two comrades were surrounded.

'All right,' the leader of the party said, brandishing his Colt. 'Come out of there — the three uv yuh. The boss wants yuh.'

There was nothing for it but to obey. Milford emerged slowly, his hands up, and his two comrades followed. They did not say anything as their weapons were taken from them and they were ordered to remount their horses. Before long they were back in town and were taken straight to the Yellow Nugget. In the main pool room M'Cloud was waiting. He gave a grim smile when he saw the three men led in.

'Clever, wusn't yuh?' he asked briefly. 'Thought yuh could git away in time! I'm not *that* loco! I reckon yuh had only one idea in mind, Marshal — to lift that gold I've hidden.'

'Where's Chris?' Milford asked, ignoring the question.

'None uv yuh business. Chris belongs to me, whether yuh like it or not . . . Anyways,' M'Cloud continued, thinking, 'I've bin givin' some thought as t' what I might do with yuh and these two boys of yourn. I'd figgered on a hangin', but there's a better way.'

'Like burning us to death, mebbe?' one of Milford's men asked.

'Nope. Gettin' yuh shot down as outlaws.'

Milford frowned. 'What the devil are you driving at, M'Cloud? You don't suppose the stage coach driver or his ramrod would shoot down a marshal, do you?'

'Not if he *knew* who he wus shootin', no. But if he don't he'd just shoot — an' leave it at that . . . I've just had the tip-off over the telegraph frum one of my boys in Topeka that there's a special stage heading for Dodge City today. It won't have any gold on it, but I guess the outlaws who've bin doin' the robberies ain't supposed t' know that. My sheriff here is goin' t' send telegraphic infurmation to Topeka to warn them that he has news that bandits will again hold up the stage at a certain point. That will mean the boys on the driving box'll be ready for it — and they'll let all hell loose the minnit they see masked outlaws waitin' for 'em.'

M'Cloud stopped and grinned. 'In other words, fellers, I kill two birds with one stone. Yuh'll have guns, but they won't be loaded, and yuh'll be blasted the minnit that stage arrives. Yuh won't escape neither, because me an' my boys'll be keeping yuh covered from rock shelter. The authorities at Dodge'll be told that the bandits have all been wiped out, which means the chase fur me'll be called off. You, Marshal, will be dead — like yuh pals. All I've got t' do then is collect the gold, along with my boys, an' get out of this region while everythin' is nice an' peaceful, takin' Chris with me. Mighty simple, ain't it?'

Milford did not answer. The more he thought about the plan the more ingenious it seemed to be. M'Cloud had certainly worked out a nice piece of strategy — and, being the kind of man he was, would undoubtedly carry it through.

6

M'Cloud was lenient enough to permit a breakfast of baked beans and coffee for his three captives, though whether it was generosity or the fact that he wanted his prisoners to be fully conscious of what was going to happen to them was a problem.

In any event, when the meal was over Milford and his comrades were again ordered to their horses; then, in the midst of a tight circle of riders, with M'Cloud at their head, they were taken to the point of the Topeka — Dodge City trail which M'Cloud had selected as the site of activity — which site was also known to the driver and ramrod of the stage, who, by now, must be somewhere on their way.

'Yeah, this is it,' M'Cloud decided, looking about, him. 'OK, fellers, fix up these mugs.'

The 'fixing' consisted of giving Milford and his two men six-guns between them, all of them unloaded. Then their 'kerchiefs were tied high up their faces. M'Cloud considered them and shook his head.

'Somethin' I should ha' thought uv to clinch things,' he said. 'The marshal here oughta wear my shirt. Same one I've worn before on these hold-ups. An' my hat. Reckon that'll make things clearer than ever. OK Marshal, yore changin' with me right now.'

Milford dismounted and did as he was ordered, then returned to the horse.

'Yuh can keep your 'kerchiefs up or pull 'em down, an' I can't stop yuh,' M'Cloud said. 'But it won't make any difference since the stage driver and his side-kick won't bother ter look at your mugs: he'll shoot — an' keep on shootin'. So it's up t' you.'

Milford shrugged and left his 'kerchief where it was. At the moment there didn't seem to be much point in doing

143

anything. He and his two companions were nakedly exposed on the trail, the useless guns in their hands. To the rear, out of sight but watchful, M'Cloud and his men took up positions, ready to shoot to kill if any attempt at a getaway was made. M'Cloud hoped that no funny business would be attempted: it would spoil his own plans too much.

Which thought was also in Milford's mind. Was it better to be shot running for it, and blow M'Cloud's plans sky high — or was there a better chance of survival by risking the shots from the fast-moving stage? He could not be sure — and indeed did not have the chance, for there came the sound of the stage on the still air, the thunder of its wheels growing louder.

In another few seconds it had come into view. Milford looked quickly about him and noted the possible rock coverage not very far distant. Instantly he motioned his colleagues and began to hurtle towards it. M'Cloud watched intently but he did not fire for fear of betraying his own position — then he grinned widely as from the oncoming stage there blasted a sudden fusillade of shots. The ramrod was standing up on the swaying vehicle, guns blazing one after the other in his hands. Milford reached the nearest rock just as the bullets peppered into it. His two colleagues gasped and groaned, reeling out of their saddles. Milford saw it happen, and did exactly as they did, crashing into the dust and lying motionless.

The stage went on its way, harness jingling and wheels rattling. Slowly the sunlight drifted again through the dispersing dust cloud.

'Reckon that did it,' M'Cloud grinned. 'Got all three of 'em, which puts us in the clear frum here on. Better make sure of those mugs first.'

He dismounted from his horse and strode across the intervening space with his gun at the ready. He knew within a few seconds that Milford's two colleagues were dead. They had been plugged with bullets back and front. M'Cloud nodded to himself and moved over to where Milford was sprawling; then, as he stooped to examine him, he got the surprise of his life. Milford suddenly doubled up and lashed out with both feet, taking M'Cloud straight in the face. He howled with pain as the heavy riding boots cut into his cheeks and mouth. The blow jerked him backwards and his gun fell out of his hand. Immediately Milford had it in his grip — and just as quickly he fired at the man who was following M'Cloud across the space. The man gave a yell of anguish and gripped his arm as blood coursed down it.

'OK, so you want to play games,' Milford said bitterly, watching intently. 'Drop your hardware, the lot of you! *Drop* it, I say — Get up, you!' he spat at M'Cloud, and, very slowly, holding his injured, bleeding face, the outlaw obeyed.

'Evidently some tricks you fall for even yet, M'Cloud,' Milford said. 'Like my lying doggo there. You got my two boys, or at least the stage driver did, but I wasn't even scratched.'

'So what happens now?' M'Cloud demanded, his eyes narrowed.

'We're going to dig up the gold you've stolen, M'Cloud, and then we're going to ride straight on to Dodge City . . . Get your horses, all of you.'

M'Cloud hesitated, giving a glance back at his men. They had their hands raised.

'Better not try anything, M'Cloud,' Milford warned. 'I don't have to tell you I can shoot fast, and straight.'

M'Cloud tightened his lips and started walking, Milford right behind him. When the other gunmen had been reached, Milford took their weapons and threw them away in the sand, rather than encumber himself with them.

'Two of you men pick up those friends of mine and put them on your horses,' he ordered. 'They're going to be taken to Dodge City, too. I'm doing this thing properly whilst I'm at it.'

Milford's gun was not to be denied. He watched every move, keeping his distance, but never missing the action of any man. The two dead men were hauled on to the horses, then the gunmen themselves climbed into the saddles. M'Cloud was the last to get mounted. Being disarmed, there was little he could do but keep a wary eye on Milford — but if he hoped for even a split second's break, he was disappointed. Milford swung up to his horse, the reins of his two friends' horses to the back of his saddle. Then he motioned the party to get on the move.

'I know just where that ten thousand gold cache is, M'Cloud,' he said, 'and that's where we're going. Afterwards I'll make you tell me where the later gold is hidden.'

'Y'mean, yuh hope yuh will!' M'Cloud gave a sullen glare.

'You'll see, my friend. I can be very persuasive. Now get moving.'

The gunmen began riding, Milford

remaining in the rear so he could watch them without being watched. They bore leftwards to the trail itself and then began travelling eastwards at a swift gallop, Milford keeping his eyes open sharply for the tell-tale marked rock which he knew lay in this direction.

But luck was not with him. The passage of the stage in this direction not so long before had, as usual, flung dozens of uneven stones across the beaten track. It was a tragic mischance that his speeding horse, close behind the gunmen, suddenly twisted his foreleg on one of the stones. The animal stumbled desperately, but failed to regain balance. Before he realized what was happening Milford found himself hurled over the animal's head and crashed heavily on his back in the dust with half the senses knocked out of him.

He twirled desperately, his gun ready, but his advantage had gone. A well-aimed chunk of rock struck him on the side of the head, and for a second or two his senses blanked under the impact. By the time he'd got a grip on himself he was being hauled up between two of the grinning gunmen, M'Cloud handling the gun and smiling crookedly.

'Just too bad, feller,' he said, watching the fallen horse struggle onto its feet and shake itself. 'I really thought yuh'd gotten away with it fur once.'

Milford breathed hard, furious at the thought of having lost everything when so near to success. He kept his hand up and eyed the gun, expecting to hear the hammer cock at any moment.

'Kinda guess this puts things back where we started, huh?' M'Cloud asked. 'The stage driver still thinks he wiped yuh out along with yuh pardners. And I can still vamoose from this district with the gold, as I figgered. Only thing left is ter decide what I do with you. Bullet's sure too good fur yuh after all the trouble yuh've caused.'

'Dump him in the desert, boss, and leave him to rot,' one of the men said viciously, and, glancing at him, Milford saw it was the one with the wounded hand who had spoken.

'Yeah . . . ' M'Cloud looked thoughtful. 'Yeah, I reckon that's a mighty good idea. Desert ain't a nice place t' git ditched, hog-tied, an' with no water.'

Milford waited, his face grim. He knew exactly what death in the desert could be like and longed instead for the quick, impersonal bullet.

'Back on yuh horse,' M'Cloud ordered, his mind made up. 'I'll fix you, feller — but good!'

Milford obeyed, swinging up to the saddle. From then on he was compelled to keep riding amidst the circle of avengers, and his journey ended at the point where the mountain trail led directly into the blistering waste which led to Topeka. Even at this point, however, M'Cloud was not satisfied. He kept, on riding into the desert until a point perhaps five miles from the recognized trail had been reached; then he dismounted.

'Down yuh get, brother!' he snapped, and the moment Milford had descended he received a savage uppercut which sent him sprawling.

'Payments fur that kick in the face yuh gave me,' M'Cloud explained. 'I reckon I can still feel it . . . ' and he felt at his puffed lip and the cut in his face where the blood had dried.

'Nothing to what you will feel if I ever get outa this,' Milford told him, as two of the men came forward and made a thorough job of binding him up.

'Yull never will, otherwise I wouldn't risk it. Yore just goin' t' lie here an' rot — like every stinkin' marshal should. An' just in case yuh get lonely yuh'll have a couple of corpses to fry with yuh. Attract the buzzards, mebbe. Nothin' like a bit of atmosphere, huh?'

Milford was silent, the ropes getting tighter as the knots were made. Then at last he was lying motionless between his two dead colleagues. His hat was removed and M'Cloud took it for himself, throwing Milford's own hat away.

'Might as well have me own lid,' he said. 'I'll make yuh a present uv the shirt. Guess that squares everythin',' he finished. 'If it'll make yuh feel any better, brother, just think uv Chris Dawlish married ter me while yore fryin' out here. Too bad, ain't it?'

With a grin, M'Cloud turned back to his horse, swung up to it, then motioned to his men. They began to get on the move, taking the riderless horses with them. Milford watched them go and then looked desperately about him in the shimmering glare. He knew he was in for hell if he didn't think of some way out of his predicament mighty quickly. Hatless in this withering sunlight he would soon become a prey to violent headache, and perhaps even blindness itself. Then there was the added horror of his ropes getting tighter and tighter, the strands constricting under the wetness of pouring perspiration, until they stopped circulation in his arms and legs completely. With thirst added, the picture was complete. M'Cloud could not have chosen anything more vicious than a desert death for his most hated enemy.

With a tremendous effort Milford forced himself into a sitting position and looked about him. His hat was lying a dozen yards away where M'Cloud had contemptuously flung it ... So he began rolling, over and over, until he had reached it. Bending down, he jammed his head into it, and it became crammed low down on his ears — but at least it was protection. He was in no mood to appreciate the comical side.

For a long time he lay in the burning sand, figuring things out, gazing upon the endless, deserted waste from which all traces of M'Cloud and his henchmen had now vanished. There was certainly not likely to be any help come this way — only by the merest chance. He had either to use his own resources — or die. His own resources? He had not a single thing about him that was any use. His knife had been taken, he had no gun, no lucifers, no —

His thoughts paused and he frowned. With a sudden effort he sat up again and looked at his boots. There *was* something there which had escaped notice, by being so obvious. His spurs!

Instantly he lay on his side and doubled back his legs until he could feel his wrists touching the wheeled stars. But his original idea of trying to use the spurs to unpick the knots was next to impossible: the knots were too tight and damp from the sweat from his wrists. So he tried a different method, and painstakingly began to saw the main wrist rope back and forth along the edge of the spur, trusting to its comparative sharpness to fray the fibres.

He kept at it continuously, breathing hard, perspiration rolling down his face and into the sand. At intervals he had to pause and stretch himself, the backward strain on his legs tightening the rope about his legs so much that circulation was impeded. But he was persistent because he had to be. He had to break free — or perish.

It was as he was beginning to think he was wasting his energy on a futile effort that he felt a sudden giving in the tautness about his wrists. Immediately he redoubled his efforts, biting his lower lip in the intensity of his task. Then suddenly the rope parted. So intent was he to the effort he sagged abruptly into the sand, his wrists flying apart. For a moment he lay there, panting hard and trying to swallow in a burning throat, then he began the task of casting the ropes from him.

Slowly he stood up, the heat swimming about him. Pushing his hat to a more comfortable level, he went over to his two dead comrades and scooped a grave for each of them. When he had buried them in the sand he recited a brief burial service — then he turned and looked about him. To have escaped the ropes was one thing: to get out of this torrid wilderness before thirst overtook him or exhaustion flattened him out, was another. With no horse he had a distance of some twenty miles to cover if he was ever to get back to Arrow's Flight.

No — not that far. He noticed the not very distant mountains as he pondered. There would be water there, at least. He could refresh, rest up a bit, and then perhaps make the attempt . . . So he began walking slowly, the sand dragging at his ankles, the sun a relentless fire in a cloudless sky.

★ ★ ★

It was in the late afternoon when Milford found a freshet in the foothills. Staggering from rock to rock, his lips cracked with heat, his senses stunned by the everlasting glare, he fell down beside the narrow stream of bubbling water and sank his face into it thankfully. He knew better than to drink his fill, so contented hinself with only moistening his lips to commence with. Then gradually he let the water trickle into his throat — and at the end of half an hour he began to feel more like himself. Lying in the shade of the rocks, the sun's brilliance at last removed from him, he fell into exhausted sleep. When he awoke it was night and the air, as usual, had become bitterly cold due to the rapid radiation of heat from the desert into the cloudless sky.

Shivering, he stood up, drawing his 'kerchief tighter to his neck, folding his arms for warmth. Now he faced the final problem: to get back to Arrow's Flight, a distance of some fifteen miles from this point.

'It's night and mebbe I can do it,' he muttered to himself. 'By day that blasted sun makes it impossible . . . Fact remains I can't stop *here*.'

So his energy renewed and hunger never a big problem to him in any case, he got on the move. The action warmed him again and in half an hour he had come to the trail which led through the foothills from Topeka. He crossed it, struck the trail which ended in Arrow's Flight, and began walking along it. And he kept on going, alone under the stars, the night wind blowing in his face and helping him to keep up his energy.

Even so he had no easy task. He stopped twice during the journey, but not for long: the cold wind would not permit any prolonged inaction. So on again, his only companion an occasional pack rat scuttling over his feet. He was beginning to feel the strain when ahead of him he saw the first recognizable landmarks which denoted the outskirts of Arrow's Flight. Masses of sycamore trees waving in the wind against the glowing background which marked the kerosene lights of the town's main street. He went on with renewed spirits; then he slowed down again as he remembered something. Somewhere around here a look-out ought to be perched, with orders to wipe out — or else question — anybody trying to reach the town. So he began to move more cautiously, alert for trouble — but to his surprise he met no interference.

In thirty minutes he had reached the town's main street and paused, his legs twitching with the reaction of his long walk. He looked about him. There were a few men and women around on the boardwalks, standing talking in the kerosene lights. At the far end of the street the Yellow Nugget, to judge from its fall of light, was in full swing. So he made for it, unrecognized in the dubious glimmer of the street's lamps.

Outside the saloon he hesitated. He had no guns, and he certainly had not the strength left to fight. So he turned away slowly and instead went across to Ma Grimshaw's. Remembering she had only known him as the tough Abe Fletcher, he strode into the hallway with his former arrogance. He did not know yet whether it was safe to reveal who he really was.

'Ma, where are yuh?' he demanded,

banging his fist on the hall table.

The kitchen door opened and Ma Grimshaw appeared. To Milford's surprise she had a gun in her hand.

'You get outa here, Abe Fletcher, whilst yuh in one piece!' she ordered. 'I dunno what yuh doin' here anyways with everybody else gone, but I do know yuh'll git a bullet if yuh stay on my property. *Out!*'

'Everybody gone?' Milford repeated. 'Where?'

Ma came nearer. 'How in tarnation should I know? *Yuh* ought to know, surely? They blew town this afternoon, whole dad-blamed bunch uv 'em, and good riddance. Only thing that I'm worried about is that they took Chris Dawlish with 'em — I reckon you might know their whereabouts, so yuh can start tellin' everybody where they are.'

'Now look, Ma, I think you — '

'Out!' Ma yelled at him, brandishing the gun. 'Yuh goin' straight across th' street to the Yellow Nugget and tell the

161

folks everythin' yuh know. I guess yuh were in thick enough with that no account skunk M'Cloud. The boys there'll make yuh talk even if they haveta take yuh apart.'

Milford made another attempt to explain but was drowned out. He began to back through the doorway, and thereafter he was pinned at the point of Ma's gun, his hands raised, as he crossed the street. He cursed himself for having overlooked so much. Nobody knew his real identity, for there had never been the chance to explain — and evidently Chris had had no opportunity to give the facts either.

Finally he went through the batwings of the Yellow Nugget, Ma right behind him, and stood looking at the grim faces suddenly turned in his direction. He knew he must have cut an odd figure in his borrowed shirt, filthy dirty after his experiences, and a coarse growth of stubble begining to sprout.

'It's Fletcher!' ejaculated Prentiss, the saloon owner, standing by the bar.

'Where in hell did he come from? I figgered he'd meet M'Cloud and his coyotes somewheres and join them.'

'He came sneakin' back ter my place, large as life.' Ma snapped. 'Just like nothin' had happened — He knows somethin' does this critter, and it's up to you boys ter make him talk. He always was a sly card — an' a murderer too, I reckon.'

Milford gave a glance about him, still keeping his hands up. He was under no illusion regarding the grim looks on the faces of the men who gathered in a circle around him.

'Well, Fletcher, what about it?' one of them demanded. 'I guess you wus M'Cloud's right-hand man. He's left town with his boys — so what do you figger on doin'? Running things instead uv him?'

There was a guffaw from the assembly.

'For God's sake, boys, don't get me wrong!' Milford cried, using his normal voice. 'I know you think I'm Abe

Fletcher — but that was only a role I was playing. I'm Dick Milford, a Dodge City marshal. M'Cloud found it out and left me hog-tied in the desert. I only just got back into town . . . '

'Does it nicely, doesn't he?' one of the men asked, and grinned contemptuously. 'A *marshal!* We may be mugs in this hell-fired town, Fletcher, but we're not *that* loco. We fell for a line of talk and a sixgun from M'Cloud, but we sure don't aim t'do it frum you!'

'I tell you it's the truth — ' Milford dropped his right hand and began to search in his shirt pocket. Then he stopped with a look of consternation.

'Now what?' another man asked drily. 'Lost yuh hanky?'

'I had my marshal's badge in my shirt — but M'Cloud made me change shirts with him. I guess he's got the badge now.'

'Aw, who the hell are yuh tryin' to kid?' demanded the man who had first spoken. 'Where's M'Cloud, Fletcher? You ought to know. We mean to get him fur the way he treated us — and also to get Chris Dawlish back. She's a townswoman and we feel responsible fur her safety. We couldn't follow him when he left because he was armed, and so wus all his men. But we mean ter soon as we can — and yore the one to show us the way.'

Milford shook his head wearily. 'I've given you the facts, fellers. If you won't believe me, I can't do any more. Give me a brandy somebody; I'm gettin' shaky.'

He sat down heavily beside a table and rested his head on his hands. The men made no move, but Ma Grimshaw did. She brought a brandy over and put it in Milford's hand. Then she watched him intently as he drank it.

'Y'know,' she said slowly, 'that *is* M'Cloud's shirt!'

The men looked at her in surprise. Milford glanced up in sudden hope from his drink.

'How'd yuh know, Ma?' one of the men snapped. 'Ain't a thing yuh can just remember sudden like.'

'Don't tell me what I can do, Tim Roberts!' Ma hooted. 'I know this is M'Cloud's shirt 'cos I had ter wash the durned thing whether I liked it or not. See that patch on the back? I put it there — That seems t'make part of Fletcher's story tie up, anyways.'

'I'm *not* Fletcher,' Milford insisted wearily. 'At least not really. I just pretended to be.'

'Better give us the whole phony yarn,' a man suggested.

Milford did so, finishing his drink between times. When he had come to the end of his story he relaxed in his chair, clearly too tired to care what happened.

'Mighty slim proof, just a shirt,' one of the men mused. 'He could ha' invented this and changed the shirt fur some other reason.'

'I can settle it quick enough,' Ma said decisively. 'I'm goin' to the telegraph and get in touch with Dodge City and see if there is a guy like this one on the prod fur M'Cloud. We was never able to get at the telegraph while M'Cloud wus runnin' things, but I guess we can now — '

'Wait a moment, Ma,' Milford interrupted. 'Ask for Mike Denning; he's my chief. He'll tell you everything, and he'll give you my number as F stroke four nine six two.'

'Yeah' Ma looked back grimly over her shoulder. 'We'll see about that . . . ' and she bustled away vigorously, taking with her the lean-faced individual who was the town's post office controller.

Milford relaxed still further in his chair, regardless of the men around him, his head pillowed on his arm. He had almost gone to sleep when Ma's strident voice jerked him back to life.

'Fur lands' sakes, it's right!' she cried. 'The guy *is* a marshal — Number checks. Name checks. And there was two other guys — They must be the ones he told us about, that he buried in the desert.'

'Right,' Milford said sleepily, looking

up. 'Now will you believe me, fellers?'

For answer the men put their guns away.

'Sorry, Marshal,' one of them said. 'Couldn't blame us for making the mistake . . . What happens, now? We've got to try and find M'Cloud and Chris Dawlish.'

'Yes. I know . . . ' Milford yawned behind his hand. 'But I can't help do it now. I want to lay proper plans — and right now I'm dead out on my feet. Chris will be safe for the moment: M'Cloud wants her too much to hurt her. First thing in the morning we'll decide what to do. I'll contact my headquarters and see what they suggest. The biggest posse ever is needed to hound M'Cloud down, wherever he is.'

'Biggest posse ever's right here,' Ma said decisively. 'An' we got more reason to try and find M'Cloud than anybody else. But right now you're having some supper and going to bed — You two fellers. Pick him up and carry him

168

across the street.'

'OK, Ma,' the two men agreed, and Milford found himself lifted in their powerful arms. He had a dim remembrance of being borne into the night, then he had dropped asleep before he even recollected entering the rooming-house.

7

Next day Milford was himself again. He awoke around nine, tackled one of Ma's finest breakfasts of ham rashers and fried eggs, and then called a meeting of the townsfolk in the main street, addressing them from the boardwalk of Ma's establishment.

'As Ma said last night, boys, we have our biggest posse right here,' he said. 'As a marshal, and there being no sheriff, I'm taking on his duties for the moment. I want every able-bodied man to come with me on a hunt for M'Cloud — not only to get him, but to save Chris Dawlish. I'd have difficulty in getting headquarters to supply a big posse because I need proof of M'Cloud's guilt in the shape of stage coach gold, and he'll certainly have taken that with him. So it's up to us to drag him in . . . The riddle to me is where to start.

He might be just anywhere.'

'There's one man in this community who c'n track him down,' Ma declared. 'An' that's Laughing Wind.'

Milford turned in surprise. 'Who?'

'He's an Indian, son. About the only one in this community. He's general man at the stores down the street — ' Ma broke off and looked quickly over the assembly in the area below the porch. 'There he is!' she exclaimed, pointing to the back of the crowd. 'Hey, Windy, come here!'

Laughing Wind, in check shirt and tweed pants, began moving. He came to the forefront and looked up at Ma with his inscrutable eyes.

'I reckon yuh know as much about M'Cloud and his boys as the rest of us,' Ma told him. 'How's chances of findin' out where he's gone?'

'Laughing Wind follow paleface anywheres,' the Indian replied. 'Palefaces leave signs large as the sun for eyes of Indian to see. I have spoken.'

'Which means he doesn't see much

difficulty, I gather?' Milford asked. 'All right, Laughing Wind, you're in charge of the posse, and I'm hoping you'll lead us to where M'Cloud is. All of you men who are coming get yourselves provisions and armed. We start in half an hour.'

The assembly broke up and Milford returned to the rooming-house to make his own arrangements. At the end of the half hour the posse of men was ready. With the Indian at its head, Milford beside him, it started off from the town and took the trail leading to the north, towards which M'Cloud had been seen starting upon his departure with his boys.

Then there began the slow business of following the vanished outlaws. To Milford and his colleagues it seemed an impossible task, but that was because he was denied instincts which were inherited by the redskin. Ever and again he dropped lithely from his horse and examined the ground. To him, an overturned pebble told a complete story. Grass broken in a certain direction, disturbances in the dust: they all added up to something, but as became his race he said not a word, merely urging the posse onwards and keeping a keen look-out as he went. By noon, pretty much as Milford had expected, the edge of the Topeka — Dodge City trail had been reached, and stops were made at two particular points where holes gaped in the ground.

'So he took the gold,' Milford said. 'Just as I thought he would. OK, we stop here for some rest and lunch, then we push on again. You can pick up the trail from here, Windy?'

'Red man follow paleface anywhere,' Laughing Wind responded. 'Easy among rocks. Rock hold horsehair; speaks much to me. Laughing Wind follow.'

'Good.' Milford gave an admiring nod. 'Don't know what I'd do without you, Windy.'

The Indian merely shrugged and removed his chow from the saddle-bag of his horse. The halt lasted thirty minutes, then Milford got the party on the move again, and it was from here that the real hunt began, Laughing Wind somehow conveying the impression of a blood-hound sniffing out the scent. The white men followed him closely as he led the way in and out of the trail, until he reached the mountain foothills. Here he kept on going, up hills, down slopes, through narrow clefts, until by late afternoon the other side of the range had been reached and not far away there loomed the borders of Colorado.

From a high rimrock the party surveyed the scene. Ahead of them was rocky country, a pattern of grey and black in the torrid glare of the slowly descending sun.

'This may go on for weeks,' Milford said, rubbing the back of his hand over his streaming face. 'M'Cloud's gotten such a big start on us. By now he might be in Nebraska, South Dakota, or just anywheres.'

'Indian follow palefaces to end of trail,' Laughing Wind said.

'Guess you'll have to,' Milford admitted. 'We've got to find him somehow, if only for Chris Dawlish's sake.'

So, after a brief pause for watering the horses and refreshment for the men, the journey resumed. It was close on nightfall when they found themselves high above a deeply-shadowed valley. It lay far off the normal trails, a gouge between high rock faces — but in it nestled a variety of wooden buildings. Some of them had fallen into ruin and others looked as though a sudden strong wind would flatten them out like a pack of cards.

'Ghost town,' Milford said. 'Must be dozens of 'em scattered around the region. Might make a spot to stay for the night, Windy, you can't go on tracking in the night, can you?'

The Indian did not answer. He was sitting motionless on his horse, his face looking as though it were carved out of teak, his eyes fixed on the rubbishy buildings in the hollow.

'Buildings being used,' he said at length. 'Somebody — maybe palefaces — using ghost town. Look . . . ' And he pointed steadily.

But though Milford and his colleagues strained their eyes they could not see any reason for Laughing Wind's surprising assertion. To them everything appeared completely dead.

'Heat but no smoke from chimney of building there,' Laughing Wind explained. 'Rocks behind quiver. Heat out of chimney. Fire in building stove, but no smoke.'

'You're right,' Milford agreed in surprise, after a moment. 'You sure have got sharp eyes, Windy. Can't be the sun's heat, either, because he's too low for that. Wonder if this means we've caught up?'

'Could be,' said the man on his right. 'But I reckon we oughta wait until it gets really dark before lookin'. We'd be sittin' targets if we tried it now. No reason why M'Cloud shouldn't hide out in this ghost town. It's right off trail and nobody'd be likely to come across him. And he certainly doesn't expect to be followed — so why should he hurry? Yeah, I think we should take a look around when it's dark.'

'Good enough,' Milford agreed, and swung down from his horse.

His men did likewise, and they all lounged and remained out of sight amidst the rocks as they refreshed, smoked, and waited for the sun to go down. It seemed to Milford, impatient to be on the move, that it took an interminable time — but once it had set beyond the mountains the darkness came with the abruptness common to these regions. Mist immediately began to rise from the cooling ground and the stars shone forth in their undimmed glory in the cloudless sky.

'OK, time to start moving,' Milford said, getting to his feet. 'Might see if there are any lights in that ghost town down there.'

With his men and Laughing Wind he

moved to a point of vantage where the ghost town could be seen dimly in the mist. But there was no sign of illumination. If there was any at all it was being thoroughly hidden.

'Laughing Wind go and see,' the Indian said. 'Quieter than palefaces.'

And he began moving as silent as a shadow, the rocks absorbing him as though he had never been. When he had been absent for nearly an hour, Milford began to fear something had happened to him. He was just on the point of investigating for himself when a shape came out of the night, and Laughing Wind noiselessly reappeared.

'Palefaces there,' he announced unemotionally, 'With white squaw.'

'That's grand news!' Milford enthused. 'Whereabouts exactly?'

'Old Saloon in town. Palefaces there with girl among them. Paleface M'Cloud there, too.'

'How many men are there, Windy?'

'Twenty — mebbe.'

'This has to be thought out,' Milford

said slowly. 'Chris is amongst that bunch, and when the fireworks start it's possible she may get hit and killed. Somehow we've got to get her out to safety before we open up ... And we also want to know where that gold is, too. Sudden surprise might not help us so much. M'Cloud wouldn't be above using Chris again for a shield if he had to.'

'One thing we might try,' one of the men said. 'Set the town on fire: that'd drive 'em out quick enough, then pick 'em off as they came out.'

Milford shook his head. 'Wouldn't do. Might involve Chris for one thing, and for another it wouldn't help us to find out where that gold's hidden.'

'Only one likely to know the answer to that one is M'Cloud himself,' another man said. 'That is, if he's keeping up his former secrecy.'

'Don't see how he can be,' Milford mused. 'He couldn't have dug up his gold and carried it away single-handed: he must have been compelled to tell the

179

rest of his men so that they could help him. I reckon the one man likely to have the information we want is Clint Barcliff, the former sheriff. I suppose he'll be M'Cloud's right-hand man now Ace has been rubbed out. Did you notice if he was in the saloon, Windy? The man who acted as sheriff back in Arrow's Flight?'

'Sheriff there,' Laughing Wind assented, his arms folded.

'There's nothing will draw those jiggers out into the open quicker than gunfire,' Milford said, 'and ten to one Barcliff will be amongst them — or even M'Cloud himself, though I have the idea he may stick behind to keep a watch on Chris. I think we ought to draw them out by gunfire, single out Barcliff if we can, and then withdraw him from the rest of the men if it can be managed in the darkness. How's about it, Windy? Think you could manage that whilst we keep the rest of 'em engaged?'

The Indian nodded impassively, so Milford looked round on his men.

'All right, boys, we go. We don't need horses for this: I guess we'll manage better on our feet. Come on.'

In silence the men began to move after him, Laughing Wind in the forefront. In a matter of ten minutes or so they had reached the main street of the ghost town and proceeded silently in the direction of the saloon, finally taking up positions well concealed amidst the buildings opposite it. Laughing Wind chose to stay on the same side as the saloon, hidden in the shadows, close to its firmly fastened doors.

'Right,' Milford murmured to his men. 'Fire, and see what happens. But don't keep on firing: we don't want this to develop into a gun duel.'

He raised his gun and at his signal all the men fired at once. The din was terrific for the brief time it lasted, and within seconds the doors of the saloon burst open, casting a shaft of oil light into the night. From across the street it was not possible to identify the men who looked wildly around them, but

Laughing Wind could — and did. He remained crouched, singling out Clint Barcliff as he stood amongst the group of half-a-dozen men who had appeared.

'Sure it was firing,' one of them snapped, in answer to a question. 'Some mugs playin' games, I reckon.'

'Else shootin' it out over that buried gold,' another one said.

'Sounded nearer 'n that to me.'

Abruptly M'Cloud himself came into view. 'What goes on?' he demanded. 'You mugs afraid uv the dark, or what? Break up an' find out who's doin' that shootin'. Mebbe somebody chasin' us or else a bunch uv outlaws disagreein' over somethin'. Clint, take a look at that cache and see it's safe.'

'Yeah, boss — sure thing . . . ' and Clint glided away.

M'Cloud stood on the ancient boardwalk watching as his men moved about in the dim starlight. Well hidden, Milford gave a chuckle.

'Couldn't have done it better. I guess Clint Barcliff is the only one outside

M'Cloud who knows where that gold is: none of these other mugs have been told to look for the cache. Windy will take care of Clint mighty quick.'

'Windy doesn't need to,' one of Milford's men murmured. 'Only gotta follow him and he'll go straight to the cache — Meantime, what do we do with these guys? They're gettin' nearer.'

'Get round the back of this building,' Milford said. 'We don't want to start a fight yet. We've to contact Windy first.'

So a gradual withdrawal was made, with the result that when M'Cloud's men reached the buildings and examined them they found nothing — and even began to wonder whether they really had heard gunshots or not. And whilst they wondered, Laughing Wind was moving silently in the wake of Clint Barcliff, his knife in his teeth, his feet making no noise.

Barcliff kept going, until he was about half a mile away from the ghost town, then he headed for a rocky region and paused at length before a spur shaped oddly like a question mark. Going down on his knees he began to dig into the earth with his hands, until to the ears of Laughing Wind there came the metallic sound of a box being struck. Satisfied that no gold had been removed, Clint rose to his feet again — and an arm like a steel band closed round his throat from behind.

He gulped and began to struggle, clutching for his gun, but the Indian's free hand seized his wrist and bent it relentlessly backwards. Clint fought and struggled desperately, but he could neither break free nor utter a sound. The grip under his chin became tighter and tighter, shutting off the air from his lungs. He squirmed, struck out blindly, and then gasped as the Indian's hunting knife plunged into his chest. He sagged and collapsed heavily in the dust. Laughing Wind looked down at him impartially in the starlight and returned his knife to its sheath. To kill a paleface was, to the Indian's mind, an achievement — and doubly so when the paleface was a man of Clint Barcliff's calibre.

Satisfied with his own handiwork, Laughing Wind returned in swift silence to the ghost town, to find M'Cloud's men still wandering about. He circumvented them in the darkness and after perhaps ten minutes located the spot where Milford and his boys were keeping low.

'Well, find the cache?' Milford asked quickly.

'Laughing Wind find cache. Kill paleface. I have spoken.'

'You wiped out Clint?' Milford asked in surprise. 'Oh, well — he had it coming to him anyways — but in future don't go around bumping off the men I want to arrest. That isn't the law.'

'Laughing Wind know no law. Laughing Wind hated paleface sheriff. Laughing Wind kill.'

'We'll get no place arguing about that,' one of the men commented, grinning in the gloom. 'What comes next, Marshal? We know where the gold is, and these men seem to be drifting back to their saloon headquarters. So what do we do?'

'Two of you go with Laughing Wind and keep an eye on that gold,' Milford instructed. 'The rest of us are going to the saloon. We'll enter it from every possible direction at once — the back, the windows, and the doors. That way we ought to get the drop on M'Cloud and his boys.'

Two of the men began moving off immediately, Laughing Wind going with them. His guns ready, Milford began drifting back towards the rear of the building in the main street, his colleagues right behind him. They found the saloon doors still open, so evidently all the men had not yet returned.

'Ought t' be a simple enough job to get in that place,' one of the men murmured. 'We've only gotta — '

He broke off with a hoarse gasp as suddenly a noose dropped over him. It tightened instantly, and he, Milford, and the remainder of the men in the group, were abruptly slammed against each other, their arms pinned to their sides. In a matter of seconds they were surrounded by a group of gunmen and the knot in the lariat rope was drawn tight.

'Shouldn't talk so much, boys, if yuh don't wanter be overheard,' one of the men commented drily. 'Kick 'em in the saloon and let the boss take a look at 'em!'

Disarmed, powerless to fight back with the rope pinning them, Milford and the rest of his men were punched and kicked across the main street and finally bundled into the ancient, dusty building which in the hey-day of a gold rush in that region had been a rip-snorting pool room.

M'Cloud, standing in the middle of the oil-lit expanse, gave a distinct start as he beheld Millord in the midst of the men. Behind him, securely bound to a chair, was Chris — still in the evening gown in which Milford had last seen her.

'I'll be twice durned!' M'Cloud ejaculated, coming forward as the lariat noose was pulled away. 'So it's the marshal! I figgered yuh was lyin' fried in the desert by now, brother.'

'Lots of things you've got figured wrong, M'Cloud,' Millord answered. 'I'm catching up on you, even if I have got myself hog-tied at the moment.'

Milford's gaze strayed to Chris, as she looked towards him with an expression of relief and half anxiety. It was pretty obvious that she had been under the impression that he was dead — and now feared that he certainly would be before long.

'Evidently yuh think my boys is bone-heads,' M'Cloud commented, grinning. 'Yuh fire off enough t' make it sound like all hell and think we can't find out who done it. The boys ain't that loco — An' where's Clint all his time?' M'Cloud demanded, looking at his men.

'You'll never see Clint again, M'Cloud,' Milford told him grimly. 'He's been rubbed out.'

'Yeah? Marshal turned killer, huh?'

'No. I didn't do the killing, even though I think it was justified — '

'Wait a minnit!' M'Cloud interrupted. 'Clint's bin rubbed out, y' say? What about my gold? He went t' look fur it, to make sure it was still safe. I buried it near here while I rested up a bit on the journey north . . . ' He came forward and struck Milford savagely across the face. 'You bin findin' out where my gold is?' he demanded.

'I know just where it is,' Milford answered, his cheek tingling from the blow he had received. 'And I've fixed it so you'll never get your hands on it again — '

'Why, you dirty — ' M'Cloud broke off as he seemed to have a sudden change of mind. 'Two uv you boys come with me,' he ordered. 'I'm going to take a look fur myself. If I haveta let you mugs know where the gold is I can't help it this time. The rest uv yuh keep an eye on these guys — and partic'larly on the gal. An' if any uv yuh monkey around with her I'll put a slug through yuh belly. So remember that . . . '

He strode out of the saloon with two men behind him. Milford watched him go and glanced significantly at his colleagues. He was more than certain that Laughing Wind and his two partners would take care of things when they found M'Cloud and his henchmen striding down upon them. In the meantime . . . ?

Milford allowed his eyes to travel over the saloon. He and his men were unarmed, and faced with half-a-dozen tough gunmen who kept their weapons cocked. Chris was bound up, evidently to make certain that she didn't escape during the excitement which had just passed. Finally, Milford looked at the three oil lamps standing on a nearby upturned crate, the side of them which turned towards the shuttered window being carefully screened.

'Any objections to us sitting on the floor?' he asked at length. 'Gets kinda tiring standing up.'

'OK, sit,' one of the gunmen answered, 'Pretty soon yuh'll be lyin', the whole blasted lot uv yuh.'

Milford settled down in the dust, hugging his knees and mentally computing his distance from the oil lamps. It was about six feet. His men glanced at him, wondering if he had some plan in mind. He had: it depended on whether he could make it work without attracting attention. He lay back on one elbow, half screening his body from the men watching him. From their position he seemed to be lounging on one elbow with legs out-thrust and head on his upraised hand. Actually, with his free hand, we was loosening the buckle about his gun belt. Since the weapons had been taken from it only the cartridges remained, and they — he hoped — would give enough heaviness for his purpose.

He had the belt unfastened at last, and out of the corner of his eye measured the distance to the lamps back of him. Then, with a significant glance at his men, he took his chance and flung the belt with all his strength.

His aim was dead on, and the weight and length of the belt did the rest. With a smashing of glass the lamps were swept off the top of the box and overturned on the floor, sending a spurt of blazing oil onto the dry boards. At the same instant, Milford twisted round and lunged into the cover of the crate as the gunmen fired. They were seconds too late, taken utterly by surprise. The next thing they knew the lamps had been hurled at them, and blazing oil spattered around their clothes and on the walls.

'Out!' Milford yelled, as his men surged around him in the flickering glare. 'Place is going up in flames. I'll get Chris . . .'

He dived for her as she wriggled and fought frantically to get free of the ropes, the flames searing dangerously near her. Milford got as far as clutching her chair and then fell half stunned before a terrific blow in the jaw from one of M'Cloud's men. As he lay on the floor, trying to collect his scattered wits, Milford saw the gunman level his weapon, obviously to finish the job his fist had started. Chris screamed, partly in warning and partly with pain as a flame licked out and seared her left arm.

Then something flashed out of the flames and smoke. It landed with a dull thud straight in the gunman's neck. For a second or two he presented a startling sight staring straight in front of him with a knife buried to the hilt in his throat. Then his gun dropped and he pitched on his face in the midst of the flames cracking the floorboards.

Laughing Wind came speeding out of the chaos, yanked his knife from the dead man's throat, and slashed it through Chris's ropes. She reeled forward into his arms, half choked with smoke, her bare arm defiled with blisters where the flame had stabbed.

Gasping for breath, his head singing, Milford struggled to his feet, reeling after the Indian as he carried Chris through the smoke. In a moment or two he was outside in the clear night air. There were sounds of shots, rapidly becoming fainter, then he realized that several of his own men were around him.

'Better get across the street quick,' one of them said. 'This dump's going up in all its glory.'

Milford went with them, recovering as he moved. When he got to the other side of the street and looked back at the flames sweeping through the rotten old town he remembered something.

'Windy, what happened? What about that gold cache I told you to watch?'

'Town in view from cache,' he answered. 'Laughing Wind and paleface colleagues saw flames. Returned to find reason. Saved you from burning — and white squaw.'

'Yeah — you, saved me all right,' Milford admitted, putting an arm about Chris's trembling shoulders as she clung to him. 'But what about M'Cloud?'

'What about him?' asked one of the men who had been with the Indian at the cache. 'He's cleared with the rest of his boys, hasn't he? Though I didn't notice him in the general exodus they made from that saloon — '

'He went to see how the gold was!' Milford interrupted. 'I as good as made him do it, thinking you and Windy here would fix him. Instead you must have missed him and came back to help us. By now he'll have gotten away completely — and probably taken the gold with him. Let's go look — Here, Chris, tie this round your arm. Or better still I'll do it for you.'

He tugged off her 'kerchief and bound it round her blistered flesh. She smiled gratefully in the glare of the fire, then held on to Milford's hand as he started to move.

'Do you have to go on chasing him?' she asked wearily. 'I'm free of him — and he'll never get me again. And you're safe. Why do we have to go *looking* for trouble?'

'Because I'm a marshal, Chris, with a job to finish. I can send you back to Arrow's Flight with a couple of the boys if you like.'

'No, Dick — I'm staying with you. Only way I feel safe.'

'Thanks for the first name,' he murmured, squeezing her to him. Then to his men he added, 'We'd better go back for our horses and then follow M'Cloud as fast as we can. He won't move at any speed carrying that gold.'

'We don't know he and his men took horses when they went to look at the cache,' one of the men pointed out. 'In fact I don't s'pose he would. How far away is the cache, Windy?'

'Half a mile as the arrow flies.'

'You're right,' Milford agreed. 'He wouldn't take a horse for that — and I don't suppose he'd come back for one either when he saw the fire that had started. He'll probably be hidden somewhere near the cache, waiting either for his vamoosed boys to turn up with horses, or ready to blast anybody who tries to get near him. My guess is his boys won't help him. They've jumped on their cayuses and run for it . . . All right, let's see what we can find out by walking it.'

Holding tightly on to Chris he began moving forward with his men around him. The drawback lay in the fact that they were none of them armed, and there had not been time in the fire to snatch any of the weapons of the men who had fallen. The only weapon between them was Laughing Wind's knife — which he carried in his sheath.

'Goin' t'be tough without guns if he opens up,' one of the men commented. 'We'll risk it,' Milford muttered, peering ahead in the uncertain starlight. 'He won't be able to take much of an aim in this light, anyways. Guess we should have packed spare weapons and ammo with our horses, only we never thought it would be necessary, and the less weight for the horses, the better.'

'Cache one hundred yards ahead, or

thereabouts,' remarked one of the men who had been guarding it.

Milford nodded, but he kept on going, wary at every step for a sudden shot — but nothing happened. He finally reached the spot which Laughing Wind indicated and then stood looking about him in the gloom. There was silence. It seemed as though M'Cloud had actually run for it at last, leaving his beloved gold behind.

'Better see if it's there,' Millord said. 'Take a look, boys.'

Two of them began digging in the earth, Milford and Chris watching them, the other men close around them in a circle. Then, before the two men who were digging with their hands could complete their task something happened. There was a sound of sliding soil and rock chippings and it looked for a moment as though a snake were lashing out of the ground. A second later a noosed rope tightened round the party, flinging them over. It slipped as high as their waists as they made a frantic effort to get free of it — then they found themselves being dragged along.

After a second or two they were pulled away from the trail and were dragged through the scrub grass towards the tall rock face nearby. Milford, in the few glimpses he had, realized that the rope led up to a rimrock overhead. He clung to the gasping girl, who had her arms about him — and the rope still dragged, upwards this time. Presently it came to a jerking halt, leaving the entire party swinging in mid-air, bumping gently against the rock face.

From somewhere above there came a guffaw of laughter, then after a moment or two small showers of stone came down before the arrival of a party of men. They jumped down to the level and surveyed their handiwork.

'Nice work,' M'Cloud commented; then he came forward. 'Pretty neat, huh?' he asked. 'I knew if yuh got free uv that fire that yuh'd come to look fur the gold fust thing, so when my boys doubled back to their horses to warn me — an' help me — we figgered a plan. We buried a big lariat noose round the space where the gold is, just covering the noose with soil so's yuh wouldn't notice it. We fastened the free end to a loose boulder on the rim above, then carried the rope round a spur. All we had to do was shove the loose boulder and it acted like a weight, draggin' the bunch uv you up there.'

Milford struggled furiously, but his arms, like those of the other men and Chris, were pinned to his sides.

'Which seems like where we finish,' M'Cloud said, 'I've got me boys here an' we can take the gold with us. Only thing I don't like is leavin' you, Chris, but I can't get yuh free without bringing loose the rest of these gorillas. So I guess it's so long . . . '

He turned away with his men and moved over to the cache. Milford moved, tugging at his arms uselessly. In the dim starlight he could see Chris's face close to his own. She was biting her lips as the rope cut savagely into her burned arm.

'We'll figure something, Chris,' Milford murmured, then he turned to watch M'Cloud and his men.

In the space of a few minutes they had dug out the two cases of ingots and were staggering with them towards the slope. They went up it, then at length had gone from view. In a while there was the sound of their horses along the ledge above — then this too faded into silence.

'Windy,' Milford said, 'you're the only one, who can do anything. You've got a knife. How's about it?'

'Laughing Wind trying to pull hand free,' the Indian panted, struggling hard. And he kept up the effort for several minutes, with intervals for rest between. At last there came it sudden jolt and the rope swayed back and forth.

'Done it?' Chris asked anxiously.

'Arm free,' Laughing Wind responded. 'Hard to reach knife . . .'

After some more difficulty he succeeded in dragging it out of his belt sheath, then he started to saw at the rope steadily as it pinned him about the chest.

'Prepare for drop,' he said presently, and at that moment the rope gave way.

Instantly the group dropped, hitting the scrubby soil and plunging over and over. One by one they got on their feet casting away the rope. Milford's first thought was for Chris. He helped her up and held her to him.

'This is no place for you, Chris,' he said quietly. 'You ought to get back home and have that arm properly fixed. It's raw and blistered, and you must be dead beat.'

'Uh-huh,' she admitted wearily. 'But unless I'm with you, Dick, I don't feel safe.'

'There's nothing to worry about now,' he assured her. 'M'Cloud has far more things to occupy his mind than chasing after you. Besides, he thinks he ditched the lot of us with that rope trick.'

'He oughta have known better,' one of the men growled. 'I guess that was the easiest scrape we ever got out of.'

'It wouldn't have been if Windy hadn't had his hunting knife,' Milford pointed out. 'Otherwise we might have hung there until we fried. Evidently M'Cloud had forgotten the knife. Anyway, I'm going after him. He's encumbered with that gold and I've got to nail him. Cliff — Billy, take care of Chris here and see her safely home.'

'Sure thing, Marshal.'

'But suppose something happens to you whilst you're away?' the girl asked anxiously. 'I'll never have an easy moment for thinking about you.'

'That's tough, Chris — for both of us — but it's got to be done. You can't stick any more of this, and the fight isn't over yet. I'll be back — never fear.' He kissed her upturned face gently in the light of the rising moon, then nodded to Cliff and Billy. 'OK, boys, you know where the horses are. See she's all right.'

This time she raised no argument and Milford stood watching her pick her way amidst the scrub with the two men holding on to her on either side; then he turned to the few men and the Indian gathered about him.

'Up to you now, Windy,' he said. 'We know M'Cloud and his boys started off from the rimrock trail, so I'm leaving it to you to discover in which direction. We're on foot and he's on horseback — but carrying the devil of a load, so we ought to about equalize for speed.'

'And when we catch up?' one of the men asked. 'Not a weapon between us — except Windy's knife. How do you figger on dealing with that?'

'Depends on the conditions when we sight the enemy. Let's get on the move. Lead on, Windy.'

8

With only the stars and the glow from the rising moon to help him, Laughing Wind did not find it easy to follow M'Cloud's tracks. It appeared he had followed the narrow trail which ran atop the rimrock, and then branched off into a cleft where the rocky nature of the ground made tracking difficult — but the Indian kept at his task relentlessly, searching here, pausing there, then hurrying on again. It was at the point where the lower foothills opened into a wooded depression that Milford called a halt.

'Reckon it's time we rested, fellers,' he said. 'We can move twice as fast by day and we need all our strength for whatever fight we may have to make when we catch up. Guess we can stop here for a while.'

But he had reckoned without the

cold of the night. Having no bedrolls with them and no warm food — or any food at all for that matter — they had to get on the move again to save themselves being chilled.

'Which way from here, Windy?' Milford asked, gazing down into the wooded region, visible as darker grey amidst the rocks in the moonlight.

'Paleface travel down there,' he answered, nodding below. 'Horse tracks plain. Heavy marks from weight of gold.'

'Good enough. We'll go the same way. Come on, boys.'

In silence they began desecending the rock strewn slope, but in the clear spaces where the soil was visible there were obvious signs of horses having passed that way not very long before. The moonlight revealed the hoof-prints clearly.

'Must be some kind of continuation to this hollow beyond the woodland,' Milford remarked, as they kept on going. 'It wouldn't make sense other-wise to ride down here. It's walled in by rocks on every side.'

Nobody commented. Each was wondering how much further the chase was going to take them, but each knew also that Milford would never give up until he had either got his man or been wiped out in the doing.

Perhaps ten minutes after they started to descend the slope they came to the edge of the woodland. Here the moonlight vanished and there was only the very dimmest greyness, blackened here and there by the outline of tree boles and dense undergrowth. It crackled underfoot as the men progressed. Then suddenly Laughing Wind stopped, holding Milford's arm.

'Quiet!' the Indian instructed. 'Laughing Wind hear other sounds.'

Each man froze and waited, feeling thoroughly helpless without guns to call on. They failed completely to hear what it was that had attracted the Indian's attention — but evidently he could still hear something, for he began to glide away, picking a path through the undergrowth with the quietness of a tiger on the hunt.

'D'yuh suppose he's located M'Cloud an' his boys?' one of the men murmured in Milford's ear.

'No telling. Could be. I suppose. This might make a good place to spend the night, at that.'

There was a long interval before the redskin returned, then he did so without making any sounds in the undergrowth. He sought out Milford and came close to him.

'Paleface M'Cloud sleeps,' he murmured. 'With his men . . . '

'Best news that I've had yet,' Milford muttered. 'Whereabouts are they?'

'Quarter of mile — that way,' he motioned. 'Laughing Wind heard sound of snores. Laughing Wind went to look. Horses there too.'

'And the gold,' one of the men said. 'That'll be with 'em. Now what do we do? Try and sneak up on them? Durn it, if we only had a lariat we could pay 'em back in their own coin and nab the whole dad-blamed bunch of 'em.'

'We haven't a lariat, or guns, or any weapons at all,' Milford said, with a trace of irritation. 'But I think we have another weapon, just as powerful. Fire! We used it before to escape — or I did — in that ghost town. Maybe we can use it here to drive these mugs straight into our arms.'

'How?' one of the men asked, and the others closed in to listen.

'Unwittingly,' Milford continued, 'M'Cloud and his boys have chosen to go to sleep in the middle of the wood. All of it in this hollow, which must be sun-soaked in the daytime, is as dry as dust. If it caught alight it would blaze like one hell-fired torch. So, supposing we set fire to it at one side — what d'you imagine will happen? M'Cloud and his boys, if they wake up in time, will bolt in one direction only — away from the fire. We can watch from the surrounding higher ground which way they are going and then move to meet them. We'll use fists, rocks, everything we've got to smash them down and nail them. Since they won't be expecting to be attacked we ought to get away with it. As for the gold, the cases will survive, being metal — and the ingots will be undamaged. If that doesn't settle things, nothing will.'

'What wind there is is south,' one of the men said. 'So I guess the fire starts from over there.'

'Right,' Milford agreed.

'And how do we start it without lucifers?' another asked.

'Simple. Just spin a rod — or mebbe Windy can do that. He ought to be an expert, being an Indian.'

'Laughing Wind produces fire,' the Indian promised. 'Laughing Wind lead way to palefaces . . . '

He motioned, then paused as Milford stopped him.

'Just a moment, Windy. It occurs to me that you boys are wasting time coming with us — besides making unnecessary noise. Windy and I will go and start the fire. You go out of the wood and keep a watch for what happens when M'Cloud and his boys start running for safety.'

'OK, Marshal; we'll deal with them.'

They turned and headed for the thinner regions where the wood ended. Milford and Laughing Wind moved in the opposite direction — and for Milford it was desperately slow progress trying to avoid making any sounds. In the main, thanks to the Indian's help, he succeeded, or appeared to since there were no sounds from the depths of the wood.

So, finally, Laughing Wind parted the thick bushes and pointed. Milford looked into a small clearing and grinned. M'Cloud and his boys were there, in their blankets, dimly visible in the moonlight filtering through the high branches of the trees. Not far away, apparently asleep also, were the horses, tethered to a tree bole.

'Just asking for it, Windy,' Milford murmured.

'OK — we'll start the fire about a

hundred yards away and then see what happens.'

Laughing Wind nodded and moved away, Milford following behind him. Presently they reached a spot where there was a small open area, free of trees but overrun with dense undergrowth. Methodically, the Indian began to collect twigs and chippings; heaping them in a close-knit pile. Then finally he selected a long thin rod of wood, stripped it bare, and began to spin it between his lean hands. Milford watched intently, and at last a thin curl of smoke appeared in the moonlight. It became denser, then it puffed and crackled into flame.

'OK!' Milford said quickly. 'You head to the left there, Windy, and keep watch. I'll go to the right. Our own boys will deal with everything in front — and the flames will bar escape this way.'

Laughing Wind got on the move immediately and Milford also changed position as the fire began to get a firm hold, driven by the wind. He moved to a point where he could see the sleeping men clearly, brilliantly lit now by the advancing flames . . . But they did not stay asleep for long. The crackling din of the fire and the whinneying of the frightened horses got them on their feet. They looked about them in alarm.

'Quick — to yuh horses!' M'Cloud yelled. 'I reckon this ain't no accident. A fire couldn't start at night, 'less it wus done deliberately. Watch out! I reckon this may be some kinda trap. Don't ask questions uv anybody: just shoot.'

'What about the gold, boss?' one of the men asked, as he swung up to the saddle and yanked out his gun in readiness for any trouble he might encounter.

'Don't ask darned silly questions! How yuh expect us to cart away the gold with this coming at us? All we can do is move — that way out, before we're encircled.'

The horses reared and plunged savagely as they were swung round. They did not need to be directed. Turning their withers to the roaring wall of flame they began dashing through the unburned portion of the wood and vanished from sight.

Milford grinned, satisfied so far that everything was working as he had planned it. He turned, to make his way in the same direction as M'Cloud and his boys — then he paused in consternation. Ahead of him sparks had drifted high in the air and lit the tinder-dry vegetation. It was smoking and flaring, bursting into flame. Behind him was a flaming inferno, and by sheer bad luck it had leapt in front as well. He only realized after a quick survey that he was virtually surrounded by devouring fire, and inevitably it was coming inwards.

'Hell,' Milford whispered, his face drawn. 'How do I get out of this one?'

He cast another desperate look around him, but it only served to confirm his belief that the fire had encircled him, already having closed the gap through which M'Cloud and his boys had gone. The only space left free at the moment was the less densely wooded clearing in which the gunmen had been sleeping. Milford looked at it, then plunged into it through the bushes and again took stock of his position, shielding his face from the increasing heat. He had to act fast or be roasted alive — and even as the grim thought burst upon him he caught sight of the two cases containing the gold. He went over to them and yanked up the heavy metal lids — then he estimated the nearness of the fire. There was one chance, and a mighty slim one, a way in which he might escape the falling timber as it crashed over on the clearing in flaming destruction.

He began to burrow desperately in the ground, hurling the soft earth in all directions, scooping a shallow grave. Once before in a similar plight, caught in a forest fire, he had used such a method, and survived. It might work again, and this time he had the added advantage of the metal boxes.

Working at top speed, he laid himself

down in the grave and dragged the soil in over his feet, his knees, up to his chest. Then he tugged the nearby cases to him and heaved at them so that they formed bridges over his shoulders, face and head. He jammed his arms down into the soil and waited, staring at the underside of the metal boxes and listening to the roaring of the flames.

The heat increased relentlessly as flames swept through the undergrowth towards him, but the fire passed over his buried legs and the metal boxes themselves could not catch fire. He winced and sweated as falling timber, aflame, crashed on the boxes and bounced off. He seemed to be hemmed-in in the midst of a raging hell, struggling for breath, buried in the maw of a brief but relentless inferno.

Then at last the noise of falling timber and the roaring of flames became less insistent, and the glare which had been visible under the boxes diminished. But Milford still did not dare to move. The boxes were hot to the touch and he might find himself scrambling into the midst of white-hot ash. So he still remained in his little grave, sucking in what air there was, sodden with perspiration . . .

And whilst he waited for the chance to escape, things were happening in other directions. His men, on the watch as ordered, saw M'Cloud and his boys come hurtling out of the fire area and head for the sloping side of the depression — after which it was only a matter of moving to a spot at the top of the depression where they could intercept.

And they did, with savage violence. They used the only weapons they possessed — rocks, and to such good effect that the gunmen found themselves abruptly in the midst of a hail of chippings and small boulders hurled at them from higher up the slope. Wherever they turned the deluge found them, and though they fired their guns at the approximate source of attack they achieved nothing. Milford's boys were well concealed, and had ample rock protection. They kept up the onslaught, succeeding in knocking two of the men from their mounts, where they lay stunned, their horses careering on up the slope blindly.

One of Milford's men made a grab at the first horse, yanked the lariat from its saddle horn and, whilst his colleagues kept M'Cloud and the remaining men under 'rock fire', he took a detour down the slope, reached the two senseless gunhawks, and quickly bound them to each other in readiness for removal later.

Their guns exploding, the outlaws reached the top of the slope at last — all except M'Cloud. He turned back on his tracks and bore away into the distance. Milford's boys watched him go, their faces grim, but they had quite enough on hand without trying to follow him on one of the riderless horses. They closed with the outlaws, resorting to fists now that the nearness of the attack prevented accurate shooting.

The fight was about evenly matched as far as numbers of men were concerned, but the advantage lay with M'Cloud's boys, since they were rested from sleep and had guns with which they slugged and battered savagely as they were dragged from their mounts and pounded unmercifully.

For nearly five minutes the whirlwind of blow and counter-blow continued. Revolvers were seized and turned on the enemy, only to be seized back and swung round. A fist — a sudden collapse on the ground — a savage kick — the whole bag of tricks was there: then one of M'Cloud's men flattened before a smashing uppercut which broke two of his bottom teeth. With him out of the way the ascendancy for Milford's boys began. One by one they banged and slammed their adversaries into submission until every one of them was flat on his back, groaning and exhausted, rope being tied about their wrists and ankles.

'Well, I reckon that's it,' one of

Milford's boys said, wiping his streaming face. 'Only thing wrong is that M'Cloud is missing.'

'Yeah — and the boss and Laughing Wind,' another man commented, looking at the fire burning with lessened fury in the depression below. 'I don't get it — and I don't like it neither. I can't see either the marshal or the Indian avoiding a fight if they could be in it. Doesn't sound as though M'Cloud's taken care of them either, else we'd have heard gunfire.'

The group of men looked anxiously towards the flames, uncertain as to what to do. They knew that without Laughing Wind they could not hope to track down M'Cloud — but where was he? And Milford himself? They stood looking, and wondering, the uneasy horses of the fallen gunmen around them.

At that particular moment, had they been able to see it, Laughing Wind was extremely busy on his own account. He had seen the battle on the slope, and had also seen M'Cloud make a break for it, every detail of his familiar figure visible in the glare of the flames. Laughing Wind waited on his way to join the white men at the top of the slope and watched the horse carrying M'Cloud come hurtling straight in his direction, M'Cloud evidently intending to detour to safer regions.

Laughing Wind took his knife from its sheath and clamped it between his teeth, then he crouched in the flame-painted darkness, tensed in readiness. With perfect timing he leapt upwards and outwards as M'Cloud came galloping past, his steel fingers clutching at the outlaw's throat. Immediately M'Cloud was dragged from his saddle and crashed heavily into the undergrowth.

Lashing and struggling savagely he discovered in a matter of seconds whom his assailant was, and the vision of that poker-face with the knife between the perfect teeth made him redouble his exertions. He butted up his knee into

Laughing Wind's stomach, then slammed up a left uppercut that jolted back the Indian's head — and that jolt lost him his knife. It fell somewhere in the undergrowth and his efforts to find it only drew another hail of blows from M'Cloud.

He made an effort to get on his feet, and found those fingers again at his throat, dragging him down once more. With an effort, his breath stopped by the strangling pressure, M'Cloud felt for his gun, and dragged it out. Instantly Laughing Wind closed with him, forcing back his arm — but he forgot that M'Cloud's other arm was free. It came round with the force of a steam-hammer and crashed straight on the bridge of Laughing Wind's nose. He jolted and gasped, his vision blurred by sudden tears. Another blow flattened him backwards, then before he could get up the butt of M'Cloud's revolver crashed behind his ear and plunged him into darkness and silence.

M'Cloud struggled up, drawing back the trigger of his gun, then he paused and frowned as the Indian made no move. He lay on his face in the flickering firelight, legs sprawled, arms flung on each side of him.

M'Cloud stooped to make an examination, ready for any sudden attack that might be made — but nothing happened. It was a moment or two before M'Cloud realized what had occurred. The blow he had struck with the revolver butt had, by chance, landed at the root of the Indian's brain, killing him instantly.

'One dirty Indian less t'reckon about, I guess,' M'Cloud muttered, reholstering his gun. Then he looked about him. His horse was missing, having evidently bolted at the sight of the flames after being divested of his rider.

The one thing worrying M'Cloud right now was the whereabouts of Milford. He had not recognized his figure amongst the men who had been at the top of the depression rise — nor, it seemed, had he been with the Indian. It was possible he was somewhere in the undergrowth, waiting to attack — so M'Cloud took his gun out again and peered warily around him. If the fire had done nothing else it had at least reduced vegetation coverage to a minimum. This whole area, which formerly had been thickly-wooded, was now more or less an open space in the moonlight, the ground covered with smouldering embers fanned by the night wind.

'What am I running, fur?' M'Cloud mused, relaxing. 'Ain't no sign of attack or pursuit, and right there in that clearing, when it's cooled off enough, is still two cases uv gold. If I can find my cayuse and load it up with the stuff I reckon there's only meself to worry about an' the gold doesn't have to be split several ways. Seems like my boys have gotten the works frum those jiggers on the rise, else they'd have bin after me by now.'

He looked back towards the rise but it was hidden in the dense smoke drifting away from the dying vegetation fire. The only worry still on his mind was Milford. The dead silence on the part of the marshal was disturbing, unless he had not been with the party at all. For all M'Cloud knew, Milford might have met with a mishap. The last he'd seen of him he'd been swinging from a rope with his men and Chris Dawlish.

'Nope, he's around some place,' M'Cloud told himself. 'An' just let him show himself once an' I'll blow his head off.'

He got on the move again, gun ready, and started to look for his horse. He had to tramp quite a distance through the stirring ash and dead wood before he located the animal. It was standing quivering on the edge of the wood, evidently not panicked enough to run for its life until it dropped of exhaustion, nor yet brave enough to return to the area of the fire.

'OK, feller, yore all right,' M'Cloud murmured, patting the animal's neck. 'Reckon you've some work to do and a load to carry just as soon as — '

He broke off, swinging sharply as he distinctly heard the sound of feet in the debris of ashes — and not one pair of feet either, but several. Immediately he withdrew into the gloom of the giant junipers which, owing to wind direction, had escaped the devouring flames. His horse he moved with him, the sound of its hooves no louder than the noise made by the approaching men.

'Be dad-blamed if I can figger out what c'n have happened to him,' one of them said. 'No sign of him anywheres.'

'Only one answer,' another man responded. 'I reckon he must have gotten caught in the flames somehow.'

M'Cloud waited, motionless, his gun cocked. He could dimly see the men in the moonlight as they inspected the ashes and looked around them. There were about six of them, none of them using their horses, searching thoroughly as they moved.

'I reckon this is a waste of time,' one of them said at length. 'Marshal sure ain't here. I'll make one guess — a happier one than the thought of him perished in the fire: mebbe he went chasin' after M'Cloud.'

'How could he without a horse?'

'I dunno. Mebbe he swung, on t' M'Cloud's. I sure can't credit that he'd be mug enough t'let himself get caught in the flames — '

'Hey, fellers,' a voice called from further back. 'Come an' take a look at this! It's Windy — an' he's dead.'

Immediately the men turned and hurried back through the moonlight and ashes. M'Cloud heaved a sigh of relief, but he still remained watchful. Then at last, after a consultation which was inaudible to him, he saw the group move off, carrying the dead Indian between them.

He waited until they were right out of sight and then emerged, leading his horse behind him. Gradually he began to make his way back towards the clearing where the gold had been left, and so changed was the appearance of the place after the fire he had difficulty in locating it — then in the moonlight, amidst a sea of blowing flakes of grey ash, he caught sight of the two iron boxes. He frowned for a moment. They looked different somehow, and they were no longer on top of one another as they had been formerly. Just how had they gotten side by side?

'Reckon this ain't no time to solve riddles,' he muttered. 'Good job them jiggers didn't spot the stuff whilst they wus roamin' around.'

He looked round for a heavy piece of rock and fastened it to his horse's reins, then he advanced across the clearing, satisfied that it was now cooled enough to permit of it. He was only a foot or two from the boxes when he paused, staring in amazement. One of them was moving slowly to one side as if by magic. M'Cloud blinked, then his hand flew to his gun and he watched intently. Gradually the second box moved too, and a hand appeared out of the earth. It was followed by a head and shoulders as a man struggled upwards, breathing hard, and glancing about him. Instantly his gaze settled on M'Cloud and the levelled gun in his hand.

'The marshal, as I live an' breathe,' M'Cloud whispered, staring at the dirty face and dishevelled hair in the moonlight. 'How come yuh there, brother?'

Milford did not answer. He was exhausted from his ordeal by fire and had only started to shift when the sound of M'Cloud's footfalls, echoing loudly in the earth, had got him on the move. Now he lay motionless, looking at the gun. It began to look as though he had escaped one fate only to meet another.

'Yuh sure have a charmed life,' M'Cloud commented, coming forward. 'Mebbe I should have taken care of everything with a gun in the first place? I figger yuh buried yuhself to escape the flames an' let the cases save yuh face ... Nice work. Pity it wus to no purpose, 'cos I'm goin' t'kill yuh right now.'

M'Cloud let the hammer draw back on his gun, and then he hesitated. Instead he relaxed again.

'No,' he said slowly. 'Mebbe that ain't such a good idea. There's a bunch of yuh men knockin' around this region an' my shooting'll bring 'em here pronto. 'Sides, I want time to get that gold outa here an' on to my cayuse back there. I guess the best thing I c'n do is leave yuh right there in yuh little bed.'

Grinning, M'Cloud came forward, but he still kept his gun ready in case of urgent need.

'I can fix yuh when I'm good an' ready to get movin',' he explained. 'Don't git the idea I'm goin' ter turn generous an' let yuh have things yuh own way once I've breezed outa this region.'

'You've overlooked something, M'Cloud,' Milford said, beginning to feel steadier now the cold night air had been blowing around him.

'Yeah?'

'If my men can hear a gunshot they can also hear a shout — '

Instantly M'Cloud dived forward, closing one hand over Milford's mouth.

'Yuh shouldn't have wasted time tellin' me, feller,' he said drily. 'Yuh sure won't yell now — '

M'Cloud got no further. In holding Milford's mouth it was the one mistake he made. Instantly, Milford's hands shot up, clutched round the back of M'Cloud's head, and tugged mightily. Helplessly he overbalanced, then fell on his face amidst the still hot ashes. Immediately Milford pulled himself free of his shallow grave and dived, his hands closing round M'Cloud's ankles and flinging him over again just as he was getting up.

He immediately arched his back, which toppled Milford over to one side. M'Cloud surged to his feet and whipped up his right fist, his only means of protecting himself now that his gun was lost. The blow skimmed by Milford's ear as he got on his feet, and he slammed back a left which would probably have broken M'Cloud's jaw had it ever made contact. Only it failed to do so. With a grunt Milford lunged forward, then gasped with agony as a stinging left drove straight into his stomach. He gulped and stumbled over to his knees, doubled up. A second later M'Cloud lashed out his heavy boot to deliver a kick in the face, but Milford saw it coming and, despite his pain, he grabbed the foot with both hands and twisted savagely. It keeled the outlaw clean over and flattened him in the ashes.

Whilst he recovered from the pain in his midriff and got his breath back, Milford held on to that foot for dear life, twisting it back and forth and forcing M'Cloud to roll helplessly in the ashes as he did so. Then, recovering a little, Milford released his hold and sprang up.

M'Cloud did likewise and came forward with a bull rush, his fists clenched. This time Milford side-stepped and flung out one foot.

M'Cloud tripped and then crashed on his face from a pole-axing blow on the back of the neck. He was jarred but by no means knocked out. He heaved up again and swung round, to feel the draught of a haymaker which just missed his chin. He hit back with a straight left, a right, and another left — and Milford took all three in the face and felt blood start from his nose and battered lips. He caught his legs against the ingot cases and went sprawling, half in his former grave.

M'Cloud did not pause for a second. He leaped down into the grave, his heavy boots crashing into Milford's chest. Milford sagged with an explosion of breath, then he battered his fist into M'Cloud's stomach, low down enough to be in a straight line. He did it again, and again, setting the outlaw gulping and choking with pain and lack of wind.

He sagged, clutching the air helplessly, and straightened again at a crooked uppercut which knocked him sideways. With an effort Milford hauled himself free of the heavy body, stood up, breathing hard, and waited. Shaking his dazed head. M'Cloud slowly got up again, much of the fight blasted out of him by those blows in the stomach. Not that Milford was feeling so good either. He was groggy from the punishment he had taken, and his 'fire bath' hadn't improved his physique — but he was ready for anything M'Cloud could pull because he had to be.

And suddenly M'Cloud slammed round a righthander. It took Milford in the chest and staggered him. He came back almost instantly, put up his guard and blocked a straight left. In return he crashed home a blow which jarred his fist and split M'Cloud's lower lip.

That seemed to incense the outlaw to the boiling point. No longer using any science in his fighting, he hit out right and left. Sometimes he landed a blow, sometimes he didn't — then he found the onslaught coming back at him with mounting fury. A fist crashed on his ear and twirled him around; another hit him straight across the eyes. He jolted, clawing at his face, and forgot his chin was unprotected. Up came a haymaker which clicked his teeth and sent him reeling. So great was his strength he came back for more, struggling through a blur to slam straight into the relentless figure in ragged shirt before him. He whipped up the last blow he felt capable of making. It struck home on Milford's nose, dazing him. Dick lurched, got a grip on himself, tumbled out of reach of the next blow, then gathered all his strength.

Upwards came his right, bunched like a block of iron. It smote under M'Cloud's jaw with stunning impact, lifting him clean from his feet. With a grunt he dropped flat on his back and lay there, clawing at the ashes, all the fight knocked right out of him.

Breathing hard, aching in every limb, Milford lurched unsteadily. He wiped the blood from his face with the back of his hand, then through his confusion he heard the sound of approaching feet. He turned dizzily, trying to smile through his battered lips.

'Well, if it ain't the marshal!' one of the men cried. 'We *thought* we heard sounds frum over here, boss — Hell, yuh sure have taken a beatin'!'

'So's M'Cloud,' Milford answered, nodding to the sprawled figure. 'You can pick him up, boys and tie him to a horse. I guess he's where we want him at last, and the gold's right here. Better bring that along with you.'

The men looked at the cases and hauled them up between them; then one of them asked a question.

'Look, boss, yuh don't aim to start ridin' to Dodge City tonight, do yuh? It's nearly dawn fur one thing, and anyways yuh in no fit condition to ride anywheres — 'cept home mebbe.'

'We return to our camp where the horses are,' Milford said. 'If it's still there, that is, or have M'Cloud's boys been there and bust things up?'

'They're all hog-tied, boss — every

manjack uv them. I guess we can get to our own camp and stay the night. Yuh can rest, fix yuhself up, and eat. We'll take care M'Cloud and his monkeys don't start anything.'

'Good enough,' Milford acknowledged.

The men began moving, dragging up the prostrate M'Cloud between them.

'How come yuh disappeared, boss?' one of them asked, as a general movement out of the clearing began.

Milford explained, fingering his damaged face as he did so.

'Only thing to do,' he finished. 'Worked out right because M'Cloud walked right back to his gold — and to me. Give a guy enough rope and he'll sure hang himself.'

'I guess poor Windy got dry gulched,' another man remarked. 'Dunno how, but he did . . . '

'Milford stood silent for a while, then he sighed.'

'Well, there it is, I suppose. Isn't always possible to get through a tough business without trouble . . . But often, for those who survive, there are compensations.'

'Yeah? Such as?'

'Reward for you boys for M'Cloud's capture. And for me — Chris Dawlish . . . '

THE END

We do hope that you have enjoyed reading this large print book.

Did you know that all of our titles are available for purchase?

We publish a wide range of high quality large print books including:
Romances, Mysteries, Classics
General Fiction
Non Fiction and Westerns

Special interest titles available in large print are:
The Little Oxford Dictionary
Music Book, Song Book
Hymn Book, Service Book

Also available from us courtesy of Oxford University Press:
Young Readers' Dictionary
(large print edition)
Young Readers' Thesaurus
(large print edition)

For further information or a free brochure, please contact us at:
Ulverscroft Large Print Books Ltd.,
The Green, Bradgate Road, Anstey,
Leicester, LE7 7FU, England.
Tel: (00 44) **0116 236 4325**
Fax: (00 44) **0116 234 0205**

Other titles in the
Linford Western Library:

DAUGHTER OF EVIL

H. H. Cody

When Jake Probyn hauls up outside the Circle F ranch, he's looking for work, not trouble. But he finds trouble in the shape of the boss's daughters and the foreman, Ransome. Things get worse when the old man dies leaving the ranch to his daughters. Then there are back shootings, range fires and one daughter goes missing . . . and while the Drowned Valley on Circle F land has its own eerie story to tell, there's trouble galore waiting for Jake . . .

HIRED GUN

Arthur Lynn

They wait: six riders, rainwater streaming from their hat brims, their Saltillo blankets shielding their ready carbines, the Spur Barb riders are out to kill Dan Bryce, the gun-heavy stranger, hired by the Muleshoe outfit. Bryce will soon be lying dead in the mud, they figure. Bryce's loyalty has been bought, but there's also something there from his past and he has a personal score to settle of his own ... The Spur Barb-Muleshoe war will explode into deadly violence.

THE CAPTIVE

E. C. Tubb

Don Thorpe, a desert-wise Westerner, is asked by General Colman to undertake a mission for the Union forces to find the train laden with Californian gold which would buy arms for the beleaguered South. Don accepts the dangerous mission and on the way to Fort Gorman rescues a beautiful girl and her fiancé from an Indian attack. But then he's captured. How will he escape and betray the South and yet retain the affections of a Southern girl?